Latifa Zayyat was born in 1923 in Damietta, Egypt. She was educated in Egyptian schools and at Cairo University, obtaining her doctorate there in 1957. While still a student, she was elected as one of the three general secretaries of the National Committee of Workers and Students which led the nationalist movement at the time. She was imprisoned twice for her political activities and at present heads the Committee for Defence of National Culture formed in 1979 to challenge government policies. Through her actions and her writings she has played a key role in the emancipation of women in Egypt. She is at present professor of English literature at Ain Shams University and has many academic, critical and creative works in English and Arabic to her name.

Sophie Bennett studied Arabic and Persian at London University and gained her doctorate in modern Arabic literature in 1993. She is currently doing research on modern Arabic literary criticism dividing her time between London and Cairo. Her translation work includes the novel *The Stone of Laughter* by Hoda Barakat.

D1157809

THE SEARCH
Personal Papers

LATIFA ZAYYAT

Translated from Arabic by Sophie Bennett

MÉMOIRES
DE LA MÉDITERRANÉE

QUARTET BOOKS

This publication has been made possible with the support of the European Cultural Foundation as part of the 'Mémoires de la Méditerranée'

First published in Great Britain by Quartet Books Limited 1996
A member of the Namara Group
27 Goodge Street
London W1P 2LD

ISBN 0 7043 0204 7

A catalogue record for this book is available from the British Library

Typeset in Great Britain by Contour Typesetters, Southall
Printed and bound in Finland by WSOY

Contents

Part One

1973

March 1973

My brother Abdel Fattah is dying in the next room. He does not know that he is dying and no one in the house knows but me. The doctor has given him between three to six months to live. Between taking care of my brother, making up smiles and jokes, and falsifying prescriptions so that he does not learn the true nature of his illness and the fact that he is dying, I sit down to write. I push away death as I sat writing what seems to be an autobiography not destined to be completed. My brother dies in May 1973 and my autobiography ends with his death. What follows is what I wrote during this period.

1

Change has spread to the area where I was born in Damietta, that city which lies in the embrace of the Nile and the Mediterranean sea. The area is now so crowded with small, mean buildings that I can hardly put my finger on the place where our large old house used to stand. The Sheikh Ali El-Saqa mosque used to be a distinctive landmark, pointing to the place where the house once stood, but is so no more. The mosque was pulled down and rebuilt over an area which possibly reaches the edge of where our house used to be.

The image of our old house is still etched on my memory and the smell of its decadence fills my being, although the house is long gone. There is nothing peculiar about that, for I was born there on 8 August 1923 and it was there that I spent the first six years of my life. I went back every summer, from whichever city my father had moved to because of the position he held in municipal councils from Damietta to Mansoura to Assiut, until he died when I was twelve years old. After my father died, when we were living in Cairo, I spent every summer holiday in the old house until I graduated from the Faculty of Letters in 1946. I went back time and time again after I graduated, and the house was certainly still there at the end of the forties, in 1949, for I came out of the City Prison in Alexandria and went there, with a suspended sentence.

Since the face of the area has changed, since the small, mean houses have crowded together, the huge mosque towering among them like a discordant melody. I never cease wondering which our old house is. Do the people who frequent the mosque, the artisans and the petty officials who face eviction orders from their homes every month, realize that their tattered shoes are beating against a well of cement which splits the belly of the earth to a depth of ten metres and which stands twenty metres high and twenty wide?

My grandfather inherited the old house from his father, as well as a number of large sailing ships which crossed the Mediterranean to ports in the Levant. This inheritance was to have provided my grandfather with the life of the wealthy had things gone as intended, had various natural forces not combined and had the wheel of fortune not turned without mercy to destroy my family.

My grandfather was not the only inheritor, but one of many and the youngest. When he came of age he was, despite the part of his wealth that had been squandered, a rich man. He did not heap up gold in sacks as his father had done – according to the stories that my grandmother used to tell, and the tale is the teller's – but his seven sailing ships used to leave the port at Damietta laden with goods. They would return to anchor each time with greater difficulty, as the sands piled up in the shallow port and threatened to wreck the ships one after another.

The house as my grandfather inherited it was made up of two wings, one for the family and one for male guests, separated by a vast courtyard which was paved with coloured Italian tiles on one side and had a garden on the other. The family wing was on two floors, the second of which was given over to my grandfather and the first of which served the needs of the family and their guests.

5

There was a room that led to the well, which was used to store water under ground, the room where dough was made, the bakery and the kitchen with the big stone oven, the room where the wood which fired the oven was kept, a lavatory and a hall which joined all these rooms. A private doorway for the family ended in a stone staircase which led to both these floors and went past the second floor up to the roof.

While the wing given over to the family took up a third of the house, the space for receiving male guests with the courtyard and garden in front took up the rest. At the furthest end of the other side of the house was the reception room, a single room running the width of the house where the candles in the crystal chandeliers were reflected in dozens of vast Belgian mirrors which caught the dazzling light and shone it back out on to marble tables, on to black arabesque chairs and couches inlaid with mother-of-pearl and on to Persian carpets, the intricate figures traced on which were dominated by the colour red. In front of the reception room was a summer balcony of the same length and breadth, from which one went down a few stairs into the garden and the courtyard with the coloured tiles. A large wooden door adorned with yellow brass roses, which was considered the main door to the house, led to the guest wing. In this house, which was at one time vibrant with a life I do not know and which I now build from my grandmother's stories, my father was born, as were my brothers, Abdel Fattah and Mohamed, and my sister, Safiyya. I was born there too.

When I was a child, my grandmother told me two kinds of stories: stories about the *jinn* and demons and Clever Hassan and stories about my father's boyhood and youth in the old house. Both kinds of stories demanded of me the mental endeavour demanded of anyone who reads or listens to a story, which Coleridge calls 'the suspension of disbelief'.

My grandmother's eye and the magic of the story have only to slip from me for disbelief to take over. It is hard for me to reconcile the life my grandmother paints of the old house with the life I know, and it is impossible for me to reconcile my father, whose utter silence dictates silence to all who are in the house, with the handsome devil in love with life who looks out at me from my grandmother's stories, eager for the future and filled with a yearning desire with which he races against time. I tend to believe that my grandmother was slightly confused and that the fiery boy and the youth brimming with vitality of whom she speaks may be Clever Hassan himself, or anyone other than my father. The Clever one who was supposed to be my father climbs on top of the cupboard and sets the six-sided fez upon his head, insisting that he is Napoleon; he goes downstairs not by the steps, like other God-fearing mortals, but sliding down the wooden banister, crying 'Allez-oop!' and drops anchor in the port of the stairwell; he walks along the washing line on the roof, carrying a white sheet in each hand, and scales the mast pole at the end of his trip to unfurl the sails in readiness for setting out to sea. When the men and women of the house pursued him, to give him castor oil or force him to do something he did not want to do, he would stay one step ahead of them. They never caught up with him. He would vanish, then appear again to spur on the chase whenever it flagged, finally erupting on to the street when he was on the point of being – which he never quite was – surrounded.

Now my grandmother's cane rises and falls and the handsome devil, with his matchless good looks and mischievous spirit, leaps like an acrobat over the cane and falls, twisting around it and slipping away. Every time, the cane fails to strike and the women, the

7

Ethiopian servants and the maids, gather in the hall to watch the spectacle, smiling and encouraging the handsome devil. The dough rises in the tubs, the sweet milky dishes of *Umm Ali* scorch in the oven and the boy grows up and continues to gather with the women at an age when he should not. His father does not restrain him, and the brazen women stuff his mouth with hot pastries filled with cream and honey, and stuff his ears with whispers. They hide him from my grandmother's eyes under their cloaks, behind the sacks of flour and piles of wood, they stifle their laughter and suppress it, their bodies shaking until they almost fall apart. The wood crackles in the oven, the flame burns, the boy grows up and, were it not for God's protecting hand, he would have been quite ruined. He began to frequent the reception room where people mill, where glasses are filled and banquets stretch on every night until day-break. His father does not interfere and the men do not hold back: if the boy does not argue with them, they argue with him; they bring out the man in him; they throw him jokes as one might throw a ball, their laughter rising, encouraging him as he catches each one and throws it back, one after the other.

The men treat the boy as if he were a man; they tell tales about the sea and ports and open his eyes before his time to a world other than this world, to blonde women, brown women, to yellow, red, blue, disasters of all hues. The boy is drunk every night without wine. He swears he will not go back to school the next day, that he will set sail on the first of his father's ships to set sail, as his elder brother did before him. My grandmother locks the door on him so that he will study, so that God will show him the smooth path and keep him from the path of regret, but the boy melts like smoke from the bolted room and, were it not for his falling and wounding himself once as he slipped along the drainpipes that joined his room to the reception room, she would not have known how he used to evaporate.

The world changes. The boy, stubborn as a bull like his father, does not understand. He dreams, sleeping and waking, of the sea, of distant ports; he loves late nights, talk, laughter, women and beer. Matters overtake my grandmother and she hardly knows from where to ward off the danger, for girls from the ends of town came to the house to tease the boy; they gather in the neighbourhood queue which meets outside the house every morning and fill their jars with sweet water from the well tap, unlike any other in town, showing the boy, as he supervises the well tap, the sort of charms that would seduce even the devout instead of the worshipper of God. However, the boy, God bless him, colours like a chameleon. In front of strangers he appears with the dignity of a man of fifty and restrains the long queue of girls and women that stretches in front of the main door across the entrance hall and into the hall leading to the well room. Each one would sigh after she had filled her clay pot, her earthenware jar or her jerry-can, and called on God to make the little master's house remain a source of good and giving.

Like Scheherazade when she stops telling her stories in the morning, my grandmother stops whenever my father's voice rises in the next-door room, quivering with his favourite plea as he turns to God with the film of tears which never left his eyes: 'God, I ask not that the judgement be repealed, but that you be kind in it."

My uncle's voice rises, telling his proud, defiant wife how he met the governor, solved problems and settled disputes, and my grandfather laughs, pure laughter, like a baby. My grandmother's face darkens and she makes a gesture with her slender veined hand that takes in my father, my uncle and my grandfather, and she completes the story, cloaking herself in that look which both held me captive and made me afraid when I was a child.

My grandmother says that she asked for nothing from God save that the fate of her sons be other than their father's, and that she forbade prayer the day my father set sail on one of his father's ships, when he was sixteen years old. She had known from the outset that the world had changed, that my grandfather's ships would be wrecked, one after the other, in the shallow port within his sight and the sight of his sons, and that catastrophe was inevitable, even if my grandfather's ships were not wrecked.

Before my grandmother turned to God with this plea, the agricultural land which she had inherited from her family had been converted into ships that rocked on the waves and crumbled in the shallow port. Her family banded together against my grandfather to convince him to turn his hand to a sphere other than the sea, where the sands settle in the shallow ports, or to exchange commerce for land and agriculture, or a mechanized project. But my grandfather mocked my grandmother's family one after the other, knowing that her family were not to be trifled with, for they were the masters of the town, owners of the factory which manufactured textiles and of the agricultural land.

When my grandfather's first ship was wrecked, my grandmother's request to God became more sharply defined and more pressing, and was confined to keeping her youngest son – that is, my father – from the destiny of his father and brother. This was not a difficult thing to grant, as my grandmother says, for her youngest son was blessed with an unrivalled intelligence and God was supposed to make things easy for him; he was supposed to understand that the world changes and to face this challenge. Her eldest son was a carbon copy of his father: he rose out of every difficulty like a hair from dough and attributed every disaster to the evil eye or the casting of a malicious spell. He wakes up, self-satisfied, cursing this treacherous life which gives only to the ignoble, and telling tales, as if he were King Solomon enchanting women and men with his stories and jokes, as if he were our Lord Yusuf, peace be upon him, looking like a sultan, feeling happy as a sultan, even if he was penniless. All his life he was addicted to the sea and from it he reaped only sterility, for he lost the ability to father children, as my grandmother confirms, during an accident in which he looked certain to drown. Despite that, he went back to sailing.

When my grandfather's second ship was wrecked, on the sandbar in the port, my grandmother's cousin, who owned the textile factory in Damietta, burst out and said:

'Ayusha, the world has changed. Your husband is blind, a blind bull who neither hears nor sees. Your husband's boats are sailing boats and they are no longer worth an onion. Whether or not the port is silting up, boats nowadays run on . . .'

When my grandmother reaches this point in the story she always stumbles for she has completely forgotten what it is that boats run on. I try to complete her phrase, since I know the answer, but she does not hear me. That look is in her eyes which held me captive and made me afraid at the same time. With that look, she confirms that the world has changed, that the boats and the factory and everything works by that smut whose name she has forgotten, that her cousin made my father understand this fact time and time again, encouraged him to complete his studies in the Faculty of Engineering and promised to send him abroad to study and become a big boss in the textile factory. But my father, although he was clever, did not understand, did not learn his lesson, and carried on slipping off to the reception room and from there to the sea. He would sit with the sea merchants

11

every night, scoffing at the 'green' men who had seen enough of the sea and now relied like old women on buying land, men whose senses, unable to seize the glitter of gold or the sparkle of diamonds, emeralds, rubies and cornelian, made do with the touch of worn silver. My father stayed up all night, cracking jokes with the wags, making fun of the textile factory in town, which was the most novel of novelties, the most fabulous of fables, the most foolish of follies and the certain road to ruin, as they believed. The sound of laughter rises in the reception room. The factory is the joke of the night, every night, the men leap on to the benches, the sound of laughter rises higher, the candles flicker in the chandeliers and threaten to go out as the paint flakes, fall piece by piece, off the walls of the old house.

My grandmother used to tell us her stories about the old house when it was at its peak when it was in decline, about her husband when he was at work when he was staying up late in the reception room, about her daughter when she wore her wedding veil when she was wrapped in her shroud the day her first daughter let out her first cry, about my grandfather's boats when they set out, sails fluttering when they were wrecked on the sandbar in the port, and about my grandfather's return with my father and uncle, devastated, after they had salvaged all that could be salvaged from the boat that had crumbled to pieces in the port, with the same neutrality that Brecht demands of his actors on the stage. Brecht used to say to his wife, his leading lady, on whose performance he brought down the curtain one day because she showed a response: 'Do not respond and do not act the heroine. Imagine you are sitting with a girlfriend, chatting, and that you are picking up a cigarette that you put aside earlier, having told your friend a story that happened to another woman, not to yourself.'

12

My grandmother was not in need of any stage directions. She never used to respond at all. She used to pick up the shirt that she had been mending, my grandfather's or my father's or my brother's shirt, after telling a story as if it had happened not to her but to another woman.

My grandmother used to tell stories with complete neutrality, with that look in her eyes. I became aware of what that look meant only when I saw it, some time later, in the eyes of a statue of a woman in the Natural History Museum in London. It was the look I saw in my father's eyes the day I surprised him, in his room, and caught him off guard with the mask down. I saw the same look years after that when we were gathered around my father's bed, green youths and children, bringing the mirror to his mouth to see if he was still breathing. The mirror did not cloud over because the dead do not breathe.

I stood for a long while in the Natural History Museum in front of a statue, a self-portrait of the sculptor and his wife. My eyes went from the husband to the wife and back again, thoroughly appreciating and amused by the difference between the two characters. The sculptor was a plump, jolly man and, in his clothes and his posture, in his body, his gestures and his features, there was something of a show, a contrived claim to strength. The look of complete self-satisfaction in his eyes was the sort one sees only in the eyes of a child or an idiot. The sculptor's wife was small, drawn, fine-veined and thin like my grandmother, a scarf draped over her head the way my grandmother draped hers, averting her shining face, her forehead broad and her features delicate and refined. Any sense of amusement evaporated as my eyes were riveted to the look that I saw in the woman's eyes: my grandmother's look, my father's dying look, the look of someone who knows and accepts everything, for

whom there remains nothing that they wish or fear to
know.

In the garden of our old house there was a barren guava
tree which screened off the garden and street from the
window of my room, which was once my grandmother's
room. Every year my father would dig the garden over
with manure and wait, and every year the tree would
blossom but not bear fruit. After my father was plucked
from his house and his town, after he began moving
from governorate to governorate because of his work,
he stopped digging the garden over with manure and
the tree no longer even blossomed. It took me a long
time to accept that I would not wake up some day to
put my hand out of the window and pluck a guava. I
found it impossible to believe that the guava tree would
not bear fruit when the wild flowers were splitting apart
the damp walls of the house. I waited for the miracle
for years and years as I watched the twining limbs and
the green leaves reflect dozens of shadows from the
greenery in the darkening twilight, the glare of the sun,
the violet of the sunset, as the tree grew taller, spread
wider, grew older and more splendid with each passing
day.
    After my father died, I stopped going down into the
garden, even though I used to spend the entire summer
holiday at the old house. Perhaps, after I grew up, I
discovered that it was not a garden at all but a pasture of
weeds for little garden snakes and, perhaps, the decline
in material circumstances had reached a point where it
became impossible to sustain the attempt to keep
things, even superficially, the way they were in the old
house.

The architecture of the house which I remember is
different from that which my grandfather knew. Unable

to build a separate house for each of his sons as his own father had done, my grandfather had to add new buildings on to the old any way he could, whenever one of his relatives' female kin was widowed or whenever one of his sons grew up and married. This was not easy in a house that was not built to be added to, a merchant's house of which one-third was used for living quarters and the rest for guests and to serve the needs of guests. That is how the architecture, which I remember as a meeting place of contrasts, came to be. At the same moment that it suggested vastness, a sense of loss and isolation, it also gave the impression of being crowded to choking point.

My grandfather began to add lengthways to the space given over to living quarters. The extension ended up with a third floor made up of three small flats that rose and fell from one another by a number of stairs and which completely disappeared from one another along sinuous, winding corridors.

The way to the roof had to be blocked off for the extension, so the stone staircase no longer led to the roof, as it used to in my father's childhood. The only way out on to the roof came to be via one of the windows in one of the three flats, which had a stone sill that was used as a seat. Of course, my grandfather did not know that he would end up living in the flat which he had built for the poor widow of one of his relatives.

When it was no longer possible to extend the house lengthways, it had to be added on to widthways. My grandfather built a residential floor above the reception room, to the far left of the space given over to the house. Reality demanded that a new stone staircase be built in the courtyard or in the garden to join the new floor, set aside for my paternal uncle's marriage, to the reception room. Reality also required that both be used for residential purposes, since the original reason for which the reception room was built was over and done with, or almost. But reality is one thing and my family's surrender to reality is another.

In order to keep things the way they were, my grandfather pulled off an architectural miracle, the ugliness of which perhaps prevented it from being listed as the eighth wonder of the world. He joined the new floor on the far left with the stone staircase set aside for the family on the far right by a long hallway, suspended in the air without pillars, that stretched the length of the courtyard and the garden. In order for this hanging bridge not to turn into a dark tunnel, my grandfather built half the wall overlooking the garden of coloured glass that reflected thousands of shadows, which changed shape with the changing breeze and the shades of light and dark, and echoed the emotional state of whoever was crossing the hallway.

From the glass in the hallway at night, phantoms looked out at me.

I was not destined to benefit from the new way out on to the roof which the hanging hallway created. One of my first recollections is of finding a snake clinging to the wooden staircase, next to my uncle's flat, which led to the roof. Perhaps it is still clinging to one of the mean little houses that stands where our house once stood.

My grandmother told me in one of her tales that in the past they had made a number of attempts to get rid of the snake, although they never succeeded. Each time, the snake-charmer would come, invoke the name and power of God and bring the snake out of the crack. He would throw it into a sack and Nanny Halim, our nurse and the last in the line of Ethiopian servants in our family, would shriek with joy. Each time, the snake would peer out from the crack the next day.

I do not believe that my family made any serious

attempt to get rid of the snake. In any case, when I was born the snake was living, without the slightest trouble, in the wooden staircase that led to the roof. The first lesson I learned as a child was that danger lay in this place, and that I was safe as long as I did not try to go up those stairs, because the snake stayed where he was and troubled only those who troubled him by setting foot in the stairwell.

When I was a child, this used to make me cross. I was obliged, for fear of the snake, to sneak out from my grandfather's window each time I wanted to get on to the roof. This was not easy, for my grandmother was always pacing up and down, like a sentry, and my grandfather hardly ever left the stone seat which I had to climb on to so that I could make the leap from the window-ledge. Of course, this meant that I had to wheel and deal to get out on to the roof which, as a child, I liked better than the garden.

On the roof I burst out laughing and singing without the echo of my laughter and song surrounding me, without the walls of the ancient house returning their echo, without anyone in the house hearing me laugh and sing and scolding me. I jump and skip, I leap higher and higher until my head almost touches the sky and nobody sees me and stops me. My voice does not come back to me, the wind carries it and takes it all over town, I see more and more of the town as I skip higher and higher over the rope. When I am leaping as high as I can and finally see the Nile, I find myself singing my favourite childhood song:

> Egypt, have no fear,
> This talk is all hot air.
> We're the girl guides,
> Our father is Saad Pasha,
> Our mother is Safiyya Hanim.

17

As I get to know Damietta, and through Damietta Eygpt, I can see it and touch it and hear its pulse, I smell it and taste it; I see it in everything I loved, everyone I loved and everything which I long to see and love again. Egypt is no longer that abstract thing which I am not physically aware of, like the Holy Night in Ramadan, for which I waited on the roof year after year and which did not come to me; like the two angels of good and evil who, I felt as a child, confined me by being on my shoulders, noting down my good deeds and my bad deeds. I doubted their existence purely because my mother told me that neither of the angels went to the lavatory. I often wondered how it was that the records of penalty and punishment could be completed when a person could commit whatever evil deeds he wished in lavatories. This was before I grew up and came to imagine that I had completely managed to leave the two angels behind me, out of the reckoning.

Thus I loved the roof when I was a child, although the presence of the snake and the difficulty of slipping out of my grandfather's window often thwarted my insistent desire to go out on to it.

In my life I have moved to many houses, staying anything from a single day to many years. At one time, the City Prison was my home.

After leaving our old house when I was six years old, I moved with my father and my family to two places in Mansoura. In Assiut, we did not have time to move from one home to another for my father died, when I was twelve years old, in the place where we first lived. In Cairo, where I settled with my mother and sister and brothers after my father's death, we were destined to move from house to house.

When I married for the first time, a new phase of moving house began, this time prompted by the fact that the political police were continually in pursuit of my husband, or me, or both of us. Between 1948 and 1949 we moved to five places, the last of which was my house in the Sidi Bishr desert, which is no longer a desert. The police closed up the house and put wax seals on the doors. As well as the major moves I had to make in this period, when the pursuit became violent, I had to move by night from place to place until I found my home, in prison, in March 1949. My moving this time was not a matter of choice.

Nor was my moving a matter of choice when I went from place to place with my second husband. I think that during my second marriage, which began in 1952 and lasted for thirteen years, I lost the ability to choose to move, to act, to do anything – for a long time. The rhythm of moving from place to place, which had begun so fast, slackened, then stopped for a short while. It was not financial reasons, or pursuit by the police, that forced us to move house. My second husband used to say, as justification for going from one place to another: 'I want the best for you, my darling.' His darling wept as they left their house after less than three years, realizing that there was nothing better waiting for her. When she finally left his house in June 1965 – on her way back to her family's house, proving by doing so that the world is round, or at least that her life was taking a circular path – she learned that he had settled when he found a place that was suitably dazzling, suitably impressive for his many private and public activities.

From every one of these places, even the prison, even those which I had to change every night, I came out with a lot, and in each one I also left a lot of that perpetually changing person who was and who will be. But the strange thing is that when I think about what a house is, in the sense of a home, I rank all these places as just stopping points. The fact remains that I have no home and that I have only ever had two homes in my life, the old house and the house which the police sealed up with wax in the Sidi Bishr desert in March 1949.

The old house was my fate and my heritage. The house at Sidi Bishr was my creation and my choice. Perhaps because the two have made up an indivisible part of my being, perhaps because I belonged to them both to the same degree and never managed to prefer one or other, the course of my life was distorted in the end.

I reckoned between 1943 and 1949, that I had settled this inner dispute of mine in favour of a reality of my creation and my choice. I was mistaken. I reckoned during my second marriage, from 1952 to 1965, that I was finished and that the dispute was settled, despite me, in favour of the old house. I was mistaken again, for my house overlooking the sea at Sidi Bishr is still alive in my life.

Because my house in Sidi Bishr had been destroyed, because the apricot tree whose delicate, pure white flowers burst out from rough, bare twigs full of knots had been destroyed, because the sun no longer sparkled like stars on the pond where the coloured fish danced like tongues of the rainbow, and because the crowned moon no longer shone, trembling, from the middle of the pond and the branches of the trees in the garden no longer embraced it tenderly, there was only one place left for me that awakened in my being the college girl I used to be.

I may be plunged up to the eyes in cares, or chilled from head to toe with dull lethargy, sunk deep in thought mulling over a lecture, a talk, a meeting. I may be lost in thought, as my feet tread the grounds of Cairo University, while I wander in the grip of this state of mind or that. But no sooner do my senses awake than I find my heart, my mind, the pores of my body, my whole being opening up, embracing the past and the present. What I have known during my daily political work in the university and what has known me, with my step lighter and my laughter purer, with the well-springs of strength, of belonging, of loving and giving which I discovered in myself one day among the crowds of students – all this lights up in my memory an over-whelmingly moving moment, which soon vanishes to become a stormy longing that the passing of the years does not change.

Every one of us has a persistent dream. Having reached this point in the narrative, I realize there is nothing strange about the dream which I often used to have, which only stopped a few years ago. I find myself at night in a magnificent, luxurious hotel or ship. I am barefoot, or in my underwear, or in some state that I would rather not be in. I go round and round, trying to get back to my room and, stumbling and desperate, I go down one corridor after the other, down many corridors each the same as the last. I go from floor to floor, many floors each the same as the last, and I never find my room. I wake up on deck just as I am on the point of falling into a bottomless pit, or into the sea.

My feelings towards the old house have never been defined as they are at this moment. Now I feel that the house is connected with death. Perhaps I was not aware of this fact before, but I am today. Perhaps my fears of the old house, which gathered with the passing of time, were less acute while the house was still standing than they are now, now that the house has been demolished.

I am not imposing death on the old house because it is something new I have discovered in my old age. I realize, now, that I was compelled from the beginning by a sort of death: hidden threads bound the child, the girl, the young woman, the woman I was, tightly to the edge of the womb despite everything.

The child did not realize that she was wrapped in the hidden threads of death as she watched, each time in amazement, the way the wild flowers split the walls of the old house and rose up, fresh-faced, above the old, the rotten, the discarded. The carefree girl did not realize.

The carefree girl still gathers hailstones in a tin plate, knowing that hail lasts for the blink of an eye and then vanishes. She runs in the garden with bare feet and arms, her soaking clothes clinging to her body, carried on the wind, in the face of the wind. Her feet know the way in the dark of the clouds and the breaks between them; she flies through the air, dancing her mad dance. Her mother, wrapped in a cloak, tells her off from behind the glass in the hallway for the thousandth time, warns her for the thousandth time that there is no point gathering hailstones. But her worrying and warnings are lost among the demented cries of joy which the carefree girl lets out the moment the silver bells ring and the hail comes tumbling down on to the tin plate, the moment the hail shines like diamonds on her black hair and turns the whole world white.

The young woman at university, or the woman in her prime when she graduated and the umbilical cord was cut, could not have realized that threads of some kind held her to her past, the past of the old house. Incisive and explosive as a bullet, the woman in her prime is no longer satisfied with the sparkle of hail in the dark clouds; she would be satisfied to give her life for nothing less than to see a bright dawn, to bring on a brilliant dawn. (Authority has crumbled on earth and in heaven. With it has crumbled the pressing need to lose herself in the arms of her father out of love and fear. With it crumbles her fear of reward and punishment, of what

22

one should and should not do, of the angels and devils, of punishment and judgement, of interrogation, of the questions of the two angels and the knocking of the police on the door in the small hours.)

The woman in her prime is in high spirits in the Sidi Bishr desert, which is no longer a desert. With the toe of her shoe she kicks a pebble into the air and incites the people of the East to struggle, the day she is arrested. She sings for the return of spring in court, the day her first husband is sentenced to seven years. Her voice carries beyond the hall to the outside; the dull stupidity of those around spreads for a moment and waves of panic ripple in the dead eyes that are watching her, panic which the gaping mouths stifle behind clenched jaws. The voice of the woman in her prime rises, singing for the dawn of a free day when we love and are loved once again. She thought that the last of the bonds that tied her to the old house had broken and fallen from her along the way. She did not realize that the day she fell in love, when she married for the second time, she had gone back to the old house and to her father's embrace.

It is not a physical death that I feel today is linked to the old house, for I never once came face to face with death there. Everyone who breathed their last in the old house did so before I was born or when I was far away. When I was old enough, I found the little girl whose young mother, my father's sister, died giving birth to her. I found Nanny Halima, just a childhood legend like the legend about the ships that used to come and go from the shores of the Levant. My grandfather passed away when I was eleven years old and my grandmother when I was twelve, living with my father and mother, my brothers, Abdel Fattah and Mohamed, and my sister, Safiyya, in Assiut.

Distraught, we brought my father back from the top of the Nile valley to the bottom, from Assiut to the old house in Damietta to bury him. The experience of going back, of the wake that the family held in the old house, was indeed unforgettable. But the fact remains that the girl of thirteen faced physical death in Assiut, not in the old house.

Death was concealed in the old house itself, perhaps because the building was not a house but a cenotaph to one, a tombstone to an era that had come to an end without undoing the changes that, without mercy, had torn apart the plans, the dreams and hopes of two generations, my grandfather's and my father's.

By the time I was old enough to notice it, the house which my great-grandfather built had turned into a refuge. There was my grandfather, who used to laugh like a baby in the widow's flat while my grandmother kept busy. There was my uncle, my father's brother, who wore shoes with a heel to make him look taller than he was and who, in the elegant suit which his wife had chosen, used to listen closely to the harmonious tapping sound which his shoes and cane made as he crossed the hallway to the wood warehouse he owned, where no one ever bought or sold anything. He would come home to tell his wife, standing with her arms folded, the story of the telephone call he had received at the warehouse from the governor, the important task he had under-taken immediately afterwards and what it had done to solve the problem that someone or other was having. There was my father, who used to come back from work to the flat where my grandfather lived before, to pray and look after the well, the family miracle. With his de-liberate, measured step, my father was spruce, dapper, dignified, formal and handsome. He had a soft voice and proud bearing, a starched white shirt collar wrapped around his neck, and a film of tears that turned to stone as the years went by covered his eyes. He used to swing between being harsh and being indulgent. He was a fine man, who loved the luxuries and novelties with which he liberally showered his family. Tears used to shine in his eyes as he tenderly watched his children, and especially the boys. There was also my mother, radiantly beautiful, who used to walk timidly around the old house, lips pursed in determination, involved in her children to the point of self-obliteration. Her ego retreated until it almost vanished and she gave pride of place to all she loved except herself. Sometimes bitter, she was satisfied most of the time and clearly took pride in her children. She was strong as the earth, accepting everything and, having absorbed it, transcending everything. There was my uncle's wife, tall and dignified, with her strong character and proud bearing. She was independent, in that singular way of hers, and she was also generous. She used to spoil us rotten, my brothers, my sister and I, showering us with all the different sweets she was so good at making in her elegant kitchen. There was my brother Abdel Fattah, who was plump and jolly, composed and soft-spoken. Wise in word and deed, he was extremely fine and sensitive, and as well as having an acute sense of responsibility, he was also able to take responsibility. There was my other brother, Mohamed, who was handsome and totally, wildly in love with life. Brilliant, spontaneous, profusely enthusiastic and eloquent. He was rebellious, loving, tender, impetuous, breathing vitality in the old house whenever he came back with Abdel Fattah to spend the summer vacation. There was my sister, the pretty, poised, refined little girl with green eyes and chestnut hair who had tremendous strength and determination, for all her finesse. There was me and there was my aunt's daughter, with the same hair, as black and thick and straight as horsehair. There were the maids, who vanished silently in the twisting corridors of the house, their steps muffled as if their shoes were made of rubber.

Because my great-grandfather did not build the house as a refuge and not even as a home to live in, but as a place where he could entertain guests and where things changed hands. I gradually became aware that the old house had completely outgrown its original purpose. I saw that the main door of the garden was not open; there were no guests in the reception room, no dough in the dough room and no fire in the big stone hearth.

Take, for example, that huge well which splits the belly of the earth, which was built to be the source of fresh water for the people who lived in the house and the neighbourhood. When the government water stole into the drainpipes of the house and the keepers of the well were physically and emotionally unable to give, the water in the well dried up and there was no longer any reason why it should exist. However, under our old house there remained a lower world that stood on its own, a world of which none but the owners of the old house was aware.

When I grew up, the neighbours – who were labourers, craftsmen and officials – used to buy water from the public tap in town, or from the water-bearer. Everyone who used to draw water from our house has vanished and my father's projects, the last of which was to use the well for a new commercial venture, came to a standstill, but this did not stop him from going down to the well with curious regularity.

My brother Abdel Fattah, who was nine years older than I was, told me that his classmates at primary school had eaten watermelon at our house out of season, since my father had managed to keep the watermelon all year round by putting it in the well. I personally did not enjoy the pleasure of entertaining my schoolfriends at home and I never tasted watermelon out of season. I went down to the well many times with my father when I was small, and without him when I was big, and found absolutely nothing in it or, to be more exact, I found the perfection of nothingness.

2

I was in the third year of nursery school, or kindergarten as it is called now, when my father was transferred from Damietta to Mansoura. I was astonished when, almost fifteen years later, I met the headmistress of the nursery school in Damietta and she reflected back to me the image that she had of me at that point. It was completely inconsistent with my own image of myself as a child, with 'the tomboy', as my father used to call me, with the headstrong, enthusiastic, naughty, laughing, articulate girl bursting with vitality that I imagined myself to be. My former headmistress said that I was known as the 'tearful child', whose tears flowed without a sound. Perhaps what the headmistress said was true and I was this tearful child, but I became aware to find my tears dear. I used to – and I still do – refuse to cry in front of anyone except at the theatre or the cinema, when my crying is a kind of artistic response. I have cried as people do when they suffer strong feelings, when they bid a loved one goodbye or lose someone dear or leave a place they love behind them. But in the face of the difficulties, the problems and the upheavals which I have confronted in my life, I have rarely cried, and then usually on my pillow far from the eyes of others. I used to consider, and I still do, that to cry in the face of problems is a kind of defeat, a kind of giving in to them, and so it does not do to advertise my problems in front of other people even if, in reality, I am forced to give in and accept defeat.

The image of the tearful child which my headmistress held up for me so clashed with the image which I had made of myself that it annoyed me and I tried to explain it away logically in order to preserve my self-image. I set it in a specific period of time, perhaps before my moving with my family to Mansoura, a time at which I felt that the school in Damietta did not really want me. My father transferred my papers to the nursery school in Mansoura some while before we moved there. Every time the administration of the school in Damietta reminded me that there was no place for me in the school once my fees had run out, my father insisted that I go back to school although I always protested that nobody wanted me there. I must have cried at this time, with tears and without. My sensitivity about being wanted, as I felt I was not, was almost pathological. Perhaps it sank in deeper in my childhood and because of my relationship with my father, which, as I see it, was always a tug-of-war between acceptance and rejection. My excessive vitality was, I believe, a source of anxiety for my father as I went through this critical phase of my growing up. The fact remains that the insistent desire to be wanted, together with the enervating fear that I was not, was one of the things that controlled me for some time and held me prisoner to the need which the people I love have for me.

I am only vaguely aware of the two years that I spent at the nursery school in my town, Damietta, when I was five and six years old. I remember the school cloakroom, which, with the screaming, motley colours of the coats and scarves, radiated warmth and joy but which at the same time hinted at the stinging cold and rain which awaited me in the street. If things had been confined to cold and rain it would have been simple, for I loved the cold and I loved the rain, but at that age the road to school was full of terrors for me and, at a particular point on the road to and from school, I used to be so terrified that I had to run across the road. The fear did not leave me until after we had left Damietta.

The day we left our old house in Damietta for Mansoura, I tugged at my mother's hand as we stood in the hallway and shouted out angrily, 'Are we going to the end of the earth, or what?' and I sighed with relief as the car drew away with us, leaving behind the old house and the whole town.

I thirsted after knowledge of the unknown, pushed on by the incessant desire to discover new horizons and new spheres. I wanted to leave as soon as possible and I did not understand why we had to have such a sorry scene when we were moving to a town that was no more than three hours away by car or train. The whole family was gathered, my father's family and my mother's family, and the women of both families were sobbing. My mother was crying, her mother and her aunt were crying, so was my father's mother, and the women who wept wore sombre clothes. In our little town, where families are related by marriage and the family extends endlessly, a great deal of mourning is worn, for this person or that, off and on, over and over again, until one would think that the women of our town were born in mourning garb.

When, as a child rising seven, I shouted this out, my family thought I had no feelings at all and lacked imagination. Women in our town die in the house they were married in. Nobody in our town had travelled and the very idea was considered torture. There is no doubt that our leaving at this time was an event, and that my desire to leave had blinded me and deprived me of the power of imagination. My father died six or seven years

30

later in Assiut; leaving his home was one of the things which killed this intensely sensitive man, who underwent many dramatic upheavals in his lifetime and whom, as it does, change caught unawares.

As for me, I did not experience any sense of alienation. Every town I went to was my town. Every summer I spent at the old house I longed to go back to my school, whichever one it was, whether in Mansoura, Assiut or Cairo, where we settled after my father's death. When Abdel Fattah's studies at the Faculty of Agriculture and Mohamed's studies at the Faculty of Law started later than the secondary schools, I used to stay, complaining, in the old house after my school in Cairo had started. It was extremely important to go back to school, to my real world, and to go back on the first day of term, when everyone shrieks for joy at finding the friends they have missed, when people hug and kiss and laugh, their eyes gleaming and cheeks flushed.

I did not long to go back to my town except when we used to spend the summer, or part of it, at the seaside at Ras El-Barr with my father's father, for I loved the sea just as my brothers loved it, even if I was sometimes afraid of it. I did not long to go back to the old house, apart from a few times when I was weighed down by my wounds and wanted to curl up in a shell and withdraw, or go to my summer cocoon, as I used to call it.

My father delivered me to the secretary of the nursery school in Mansoura and left. After she had closed her registers, she indicated to me that I should join the children in one of the adjoining rooms, from which there came the sound of singing and music, so I went in. Half my dread of the unknown had evaporated on the way to nursery school near the gardens in Shagaret El-Dorr Street, which had held more than one miracle for me. The remaining half scattered the moment I went

31

into the room. The room was decorated with lanterns, with towers and houses and roses whose many colours twined together in the middle of the ceiling and separated to hang down the walls. The girls and boys were gathered around a little platform, singing to music which some boys and girls, seated on the platform, were playing on many instruments.

When my amazement wore off, I discovered that I was standing alone outside a circle of joined hands, completely isolated from this happy whole, which was bursting with joy and turned around itself singing. I felt isolated, even though my fascination with musical instruments is a long-held one that led me to smash my favourite musical toy to discover where the sounds came from, and my fascination with towers and lanterns made from coloured paper remained with me for years, until I learned how to cut patterns for them from crêpe paper.

Suddenly the third miracle of my first day at Mansoura nursery school happened and, for me, it was this that transported me to seventh heaven. A plump boy with a white face and rosy cheeks, with bare legs in short trousers, turned to me as I was standing isolated, in a corner, outside the circle. I must have given him a look, called out silently, insistently, desperately to him with all my being, like a drowning man bringing his head above the surface of the water for a moment, because the boy looked at me again and, suddenly, I found him dragging me by the hand into the circle, still singing the verse which everyone else was finishing. I gave my other hand to the girl next to me and my isolation was broken. What happened was what I always wanted, and still want: to become part of the whole. I began, delirious, to sing at the top of my voice with everybody else.

This boy became my friend for the time I spent in Mansoura, which was about four years in nursery school and then afterwards, when we established a family relationship between my mother and his mother's sister, Aunt Nadira, who became my teacher at Mansoura Girls' Elementary School.

I do not know where this boy who is no longer a boy is now. I do not even remember his name, and I do not know if he is alive or dead. But I am always him, forever him, when I look around me nervously at some gathering and I join someone else to the circle to break his or her isolation.

Our first house in Mansoura was a small, old house. The landlady, who was the mother of the journalist Mohamed El-Tabai, lived on the first floor and rented out the second. Whereas I have almost completely forgotten what the house itself was like, except for the roof, which the landlady kept for her grandson, the poet El-Hamshari, where he spent every summer holiday, I will never forget the details of the area in which the house stands.

The house was on one of the two sides that would have formed a rectangle, were it not for two openings, one on the right-hand side, leading into the centre of town, and one on the left-hand side, leading out on to Sharia El-Nil. To the right of where we lived was a little house that looked like ours where another family lived. Our families used to visit one another, and we used to play with their daughters in the courtyard of their house; later, my sister Safiyya and I went to primary school with them. To the left of our house stood a proud mansion, set further forward than our house, stretching almost the full length of one short side of the rectangle and overlooking, as the mansions of dignitaries do, the Nile. On the side of the rectangle facing our house stretched a mud wall, almost but not quite reaching up to the proud mansion. Behind the wall were scattered tents and little mud houses where a tribe lived with sheep and cows and bulls, a Bedouin tribe of men and women and children in rags of many colours. Small, mean houses pressed along the rest of the left-hand side of the rectangle. I knew only two of the people who lived there. There was the man who sold lupin seeds, wheat pudding and fava beans, who lived on the ground floor and daily carried the lupin seeds down to the Nile to wash them. He would then arrange them with the pudding and the fava beans on his wooden cart in geometric patterns, with exceptional skill, and sprinkle fragrant green herbs over them, and red roses. He would fill his lamp with oil and disappear with the cart from our world. He would not appear again until dawn the following day. The other one, who lived on the roof, used to disappear only when night fell.

When I looked out of the window of our house in Mansoura for the first time, it seemed to me that the world began and ended with this rectangle and there was nothing at all beyond it, near or far. Nothing disturbed the orderly silence in this world in miniature at high noon except the occasional squabble between the children in the street and the man on the roof and the exchange of brick missiles between the two sides.

When I found myself on my way to nursery school, for the first time, down Shagaret El-Dorr Street, slipping out with exceptional speed from the confines of that rectangle to the expanse of the Nile and Sharia El-Nil, the first miracle of my day happened. I was not, however, spared the brick missiles that the boys and the madman were exchanging on my way home.

I do not find myself wondering in amazement now when I contemplate the particular type of madness which afflicted the resident of the roof in the rectangle which was the outline of our world with its clear class divide. He used to moan and puff like a train and then run, slowly at first and then fast, moving like a train, then he would crash into the opposite wall of the roof and turn around and start moaning and puffing so as to crash into reality again.

In Mansoura I loved the road to the nursery school next to the Shagaret El-Dorr Garden and after that I loved the road to the primary school, next to the governorate building that also served as a court. When I crossed the road to the nursery school for the first time without being forced to run along one side of the road, knees knocking, as I used to do on the road to the nursery school in Damietta at the end of the twenties and the beginning of the thirties, the second miracle of my first day at school happened.

On my way to nursery school in Damietta, which is now the Secondary School for Girls, I used to have to flee from the El-Khan area, which was, in the old days, an area with hotels for sailors and tourists and which, after the port of Damietta stopped functioning, slowly fell into disrepair. As soon as the area where ruined walls stretched on top of vast, arching pillars began, I would start to run as fast as I could. In the shadow of the arches crouched men and women, nailed into place the way the vast pillars in whose shadows they crouched were nailed down. Some had legs puffed up as fat as the pillars, some had limbs, features, faces that were eaten away month after month. Today it was the toes and tomorrow the foot itself that began to be eaten away, and the nose – where did the nose go? Yesterday a bit of it was left, and today? And the eyes? No eyes. The first thing that syphilis strikes once it gets in the blood is the eyes, and the first thing that elephantiasis strikes is the legs. Why did I run away? Why did I have to run away every time? Why do I try every time to forget? If I had stopped, if I had opened my eyes wide, if I had seen and heard and taken into my memory every image of misery and human subjection, if I had buried in my memory and my emotions every single detail, I would have become a better person, more able to love and hate. If I had done so, then perhaps I would not have fled as I did in the middle of the road.

There is a room on the roof of our house and in it there is a bed with a sprung mattress which, with a pistachio-green cover thrown over it, becomes a bench in the morning. There are two armchairs draped in apricot cloth and a varnished white wooden desk, behind which are varnished shelves on which books in Arabic and foreign languages are lined up, with their thick bindings of different colours. By the window is a pitcher full of water perfumed with blossoms. On the tray where the pitcher stands lie jasmine flowers and tamarind and, from time to time, one or two red roses with their green stalks covered in thorns. Opposite the roof is a door made of glass which is always open and looks on to a jasmine bush, pots of gardenia and carnations and thorny plants that are both like and unlike the plants that are found in graveyards.

I have forgotten all the details of our flat in Umm El-Tabai's house and I still rack my brains in vain to remember the layout of the rooms or pick out the furniture. I do not remember where I used to sleep or with whom, or whether my mother had brought her shining silver bed with her from Damietta to Mansoura, with the angels entwined in an embrace on the sides, or whether she left behind her the golden vanity set with its mirrors worked with golden roses and her bedroom of walnut wood, where red lamps cast their dancing light on the silver nickel bedstead . . . In brief, I have completely forgotten the furniture that we used and all the details of our life in that house, but I have not forgotten the room on the roof. As soon as it was opened in the summer holidays, I was up there all the time until the maid dragged me out, or until I heard my mother calling me or my father's heavy footsteps coming up the stairs.

Between six and eight years of age I knew that there was a university in Cairo and that university is something to which everyone who receives education looks forward. At that time, my brother Abdel Fattah was in the middle of secondary school and my brother Mohamed was just beginning. They both used to talk all the time about the university they were aiming to get into in the end, as if it were some enchanted world.

At that time I had heard a few lines of poetry from my brothers, who invested poetry with an all but hallowed aura.

When I went up to the room on the roof when I was seven years old, for the first time in my life I saw a student from the Faculty of Letters and an eminent poet, El-Hamshari. The experience was unique of its kind and final. Perhaps it could not have happened later on, after I had lost my innocence as a result of becoming acquainted with evil, both indirectly and directly. Perhaps the experience was inconceivable within the scope of the reality shaped only by my perpetual burning for the absolute, for absolute beauty and truth and good. (Was it my burning for the absolute, or my burning desire to return to the womb? The absolute is the spouse of death.)

For hours I used to sit, me, the nervous one who could never sit still, legs crossed and arms folded like a statue of Buddha, watching that handsome poet of twenty as one watches the sun, eyes dazzled most of the time by the rays of light.

On his apricot chair inside or on the straw chair under the jasmine bush out on the roof he sits, in his pale grey trousers and indigo blazer with the gold buttons, stretching out his long legs, reading a book, marking words in his notebook, lost in thought. Every time he comes out of his inner world he sees me, legs crossed and arms folded, and is surprised; he has completely forgotten I was there and his eyes, the colour of clear honey, look at me in distress, as if seeing me for the first time. His hand goes to his forehead and puts a stray lock of hair, the colour of a grain of wheat, back into place and he says a word or two, and sometimes gives me a sweet cake from the plate, sometimes not. He disappears into his inner world again, only to be surprised by finding me there again.

I did not mind at all whether he spoke to me or not, whether he noticed my presence or not. Perhaps his noticing that I was there confused me a little and interrupted the moment of contemplation, which sometimes used to end in a unique experience that took me beyond the confines of my body, of time and space, and severed my connection to everything relative, so that I no longer knew who I was or where I came from, or to whom I belonged, or where I was going. No longer bothered by what my father tells me to do and my mother tells me not to, I do not hear my father's heavy footsteps on the stairs, or my mother's warning cry; I melt away with astonishing fluidity and nothing scares me or binds me any longer.

It was not a handsome man, or even a handsome person, whom I used to contemplate but absolute beauty and absolute perfection, until I became one with them, free from the prison of the body and the relativity of time and space, in a unique moment which ended in my being lost, in my extinction, in my death.

I have never had the same, complete experience with anyone since, even though I now realize that I have tried all my life to do so. Great love, to my mind, was the desire for unity with an absolute, it was equivalent to the burning desire to be lost in the other, to exist through the other, to lose the ego and ego identity, to be liberated from the body of the self and become one with the other. Striving for an eternal absolute in a world founded on relativity, with all the shortcomings of perpetual change, I used to feel frenzied, childish rage when my frantic attempts to make the impossible happen came to nothing. My attempt to impose permanency upon human relationships, which are subject to change, was an insane attempt to impose the absolute upon a world which is relative.

Now I realize that I spent my life striving for the absolute and that the absolute is the spouse of death. I realize that there is no permanency and no stability in a life the nature of which is perpetual change. Now I realize that for me love meant losing oneself in the other. I realize that my crime was unpardonable because it was I who committed it, because there is no crime more serious than burying the self alive. My hands are stained with my own blood.

I attained unity with the absolute on two occasions in my life in two places that were different as day and night, as fire and water. It happened in the Piazza San Marco in Venice just as the sun set, when I became one with absolute beauty, and it happened in the dark of the well of our old house, when I became one with death.

After I had lived in Umm El-Tabai's house for a while, I moved to a better flat in a house on Sharia El-Abbasi, one of Mansoura's main roads at the time. I no longer saw El-Hamshari the poet. I was not greatly surprised when, a long time afterwards, my brothers told me that he had died in the dawn of his youth and had become a brilliant and well-known poet. El-Hamshari had become a dream to me as much as he was a reality; he was the impossible come true. He was one of the children whom death chose, as they say, and his early death left ineradicable traces on my emotions, as if he were my impossible secret and my impossible dream which had come true one day in the room on the roof under the jasmine bush, the secret which always encouraged me to strive for the absolute, the dream which guided me and appeared before me time after time, like a mirage.

Despite everything, after I became acquainted with evil in more than one form in the house on Sharia El-Abbasi in Mansoura, it became impossible for me to see in anybody, whoever they may be, absolute beauty and absolute perfection. I came out of the paradise of innocence with knowledge and the rotten apple of Adam and Eve.

I first became acquainted with evil in an indirect way, which my mother's powerful imagination and my own rendered direct when I was a child of eight. One afternoon my mother, who had a wonderful imagination and was a brilliant storyteller, told me a story about the two most savage killers in Egypt, Rayya and Sakina. My mother described the rituals of the murder, blow by blow, as if she were enacting it: how they chose the victim, how they went to the house and strangled their victim, how they tore the corpse apart and burnt the pieces in the big oven, how the drumbeats in the ritual of sacrifice, *zar*, smothered the victim's cries for help so that nobody, in the police station opposite the house where Rayya and Sakina lived, heard. The moral of my mother's tale, which captivated me completely, was, of course, that crime does not pay and that Rayya and Sakina ended up being put to death, but the moral of the tale is one thing and what remained in my mind is another. Rayya and Sakina settled into my being, living and imposing their existence upon me as that from which there is no escape.

In the dark of the night, sleeping in a room separate from my mother, with my little sister Safiyya, who is three years younger than I am, Rayya and Sakina attacked me in my bed. As I lay there, I became the victim of the murder, blow by blow by blow, and I found myself running, terrified, to my mother's bed in the room next door and hugging her as I shook, finding in her arms a refuge from the evils of the world.

The film by Salah Abu Seif about Rayya and Sakina did not upset the woman in the middle of her life. Life had hollowed her out enough to make her submit to the dividing line between fantasy and reality. Life had slapped her enough and dulled her wits enough to make her forget the dividing line between a person's stripping away his clothes, willingly, passionately, in defiance of an imposed death, and his submitting to being stripped until he dies of degradation. She did observe how well the director had cast the actress who plays Sakina. Something in her face and the way she was made augured evil, she was evil in the flesh. Perhaps it was that she was blind in one eye and had a squint in the other, perhaps it was that flat body of hers which was the body of neither a man nor a woman.

The woman in the middle of her life watched the film about Rayya and Sakina and did not watch it. The terror of the child seeking refuge in her mother's embrace from the evils of the world was not awakened in her, or the girl's painful realization that the mother's embrace is no refuge, or the young woman's fierce joy when refuge and meaning are found in being one with others.

I find no refuge from the evils of the world in my mother's embrace at the age of eleven as I stand looking out from the balcony of our house on Sharia El-Abbasi in Mansoura, no one there to help, neither my father trying to drag me off the balcony so that I do not see and do not hear, nor my mother crying silently. I find no refuge from the sense of powerlessness, of distress, of oppression,

41

that shakes me as the police shoot down twenty-four demonstrators that day, as I scream at my inability to do anything, to go down into the street and stop the bullets flying from the black guns. I abandon the child in me and the girl comes of age before her time, weighed down with a knowledge wider than the limits of the house, a knowledge that includes the entire nation. My future course in life was then determined. I was destined to enter the door of commitment to the nation by the harshest and most violent door. To take even one step back from it drains me and makes me feel guilty, and when my voice is choked it tortures me. A vague hope spurs me on: that I remain able to say no to all the injustices in the world.

That was one day in 1934, when the Prime Minister, Ismail Pasha Sidki, refused to permit Mustafa El-Nahhas, the leader of the majority Wafd party, to tour the provinces, which included a visit to Mansoura. Sidki stopped all the trains from running, so El-Nahhas came in a procession of cars. The municipality of Mansoura turned streets including ours into a series of trenches to prevent the procession from advancing.

The streets were swarming with thousands of pro-testers. Some moved out from our street bearing El-Nahhas Pasha's car on their shoulders, crossing trench after trench in our street, and the procession advanced, despite everything, to loud cries of victory, the victory of the will of the masses. The dull black guns put an end to the procession and to the demonstration.

I knew the shape of events days before they began. From my brothers I learned the nature of the struggle that was going on the length and breadth of Egypt between the people, on the one hand, and the minority parties that served the King and the British Occupation on the other. With my brothers I chose the trench in which I would stand in this struggle and with whom, against whom, I would channel my sentiments. With my brothers I anticipated everything as we saw the workers of the municipality digging trenches across the roads. But they were not expecting, and neither was I, treacherous bullets from the dull black guns. The treachery of the bullets was beyond all that we had anticipated.

With the blood, like a waterfall, a deep red gushed over the heads of the fumbling mass of humanity and vanished; with the victorious roar of the crowd when it had been stifled, as wave after wave of humanity retreated; with the brass buttons shining in the sun and the long, dull black guns; with the bricks raining down on the policemen, the bodies laid bare to the bullets, the clothes turned to torches that burned in people's hearts and lit them with passion for death; with the twenty-four dead which the girl counted, one by one, every time the ambulance door slammed shut, in Sharia El-Abbasi in Mansoura one day in 1934, when his guts exploded and he was lying there, raped, when a handful of policemen remained, when blood no longer flowed like a waterfall deep red, slipping drop by drop and mingling with the mud in the street, blocking it up with coal black, the child becomes a young woman, acquainted with evil on the level of the state. The child who found refuge in the embrace of her mother from the evils of the world is lost.

A sea of youth ripples over Abbas Bridge in 1946 and the young woman who found refuge in the whole is a drop in the sea, wild joy is she and powerful, active strength, and the ego – the ego has meaning, because it has become one with the others. A sea of youth swells on Abbas Bridge. The roaring sound it makes works loose the tent pegs of the old colonialism, while the new colonialism lies in wait. The policemen chase after the demonstration with their heavy truncheons.

Suddenly the sea is convulsed and the young men and

women sweep down to the Nile by the dozen. Those who are saved are saved and those who die, die. The moment the Abbas Bridge splits in two and the side that leads into the heart of town slopes downwards, the truncheons push the rearguard into the chasm.

The student demonstration from Fouad I University reaches the heart of town; it reaches every town and village and hamlet in Egypt and the Arab world; the revolution begins when they thought it had ended.

On the banks of the Nile the young woman who found refuge in the whole sits, covering her nakedness, their nakedness, our nakedness. She sits there through the morning, noon and night until the divers have fished out all the corpses. Many hands, her hands among them, wind the corpses in the green Egyptian flag, one by one. The corpses are raised up high like flags in the hands of those who loved them. The tree of love is alive and does not die; nor does the entity that is I and the others that I am one with.

1967

One day in June 1965, with my brother and the registry official sitting in the room next door, my husband turned to face me on his swivel chair and said, in a last attempt to dissuade me from finalizing the divorce: 'But I made you.'

Of my life, thirteen years had been taken up imagining I had found unity with the man I loved for a while, then by my frenzied attempts to restore this imaginary unity for a while, and then, in the final stages, by my being struck with mental paralysis, unable to do anything. I did not wish to raise my voice, so that I would not fail in what I had set out to do, and I wondered, as I looked at him, which phase, which phases of the life I have lived has he made? All of them or none? The time I used to hang my happiness and wretchedness on the hook where he hung his coat is over. The day I recovered from the paralysis is over and the cure has required me, among other things, to get my husband acquitted of the charge of shedding my blood and to admit that I, above all, was responsible for my impossible dream, my impossible madness and my impossible death. I took total responsibility and recovered from the paralysis. Here I am, recovering, on the point of recovery, and I tremble for fear that my new-born entity will go back to the womb. I used to wonder if he was the project of my life, or if individual happiness was? This was unclear for a time, and is no more. He was not my project; individual happiness was the project I took on, which, when it did not come to anything, drove me crazy. It is I who fashion absolutes, I am the prisoner of my own creation. How did I come to separate absolute happiness from absolute wretchedness? For years I was moving in the wrong orbit, unable to act to take myself out of it. For years I was paralysed by the terrible chasm between what I believed and what I was living, between the vision and the reality, between the dream and the truth, for years, now that I have almost recovered, fearing that my new-born entity would go back to the womb and that he would turn around and say: 'But I made you.'

At the time I seemed, to others, to be a successful woman by ordinary standards and, perhaps, if one considered the work I was doing and what I had achieved, more than simply successful. But at the same time, I was devastated on the inside, even if nobody but I was aware of a single dimension of this devastation. It was my secret which I hid from people and, also, from myself for a time. For a time, I chewed over its bitter taste without being able to change it and I wondered, which of the two women did he make? He did not make a thing. I am the one who made my successes and my miseries and he made nothing. In the first phase, of imaginary unity (How long did it last? Two years or three?), I did not achieve anything. I did not want to achieve anything. It was out of the question that I achieve anything and the perfection of my fulfilment was in his achievement. Under this sort of imaginary happiness we do not write, we do not pour ourselves into a great work that requires us to devote ourselves to it totally; we live the moment instead of writing about it. When the earth began to shake under my feet a little, just a little, I felt a palpable need to write. I hardly finished preparing my doctoral thesis in 1957 before I poured myself completely into the novel *The Open Door*, which was published in 1960. When the earth really shook under my feet I achieved nothing as far as writing is concerned. The most that one can do at such a time is to pick up the pieces, and he turns around on his swivel chair and says: 'But I made you.'

I held myself back before replying: if I raised my voice, what I had come to do would fail. My decision to separate was five years old and the ability to execute the decision and make it happen was one month old. For a month I had been asking for the divorce, with hope, with goodwill, with the mediation of the family and relatives and friends, with threats. I did not raise my voice, but I also did not back down. I could not back down now, having retrieved some of my ability to act. I had backed down long and often until he and everyone expected me to do so.

At a family meeting called to set the date of the divorce, his elder brother asked: 'What's changed that you're asking for a divorce?' and I did not reply. There was nothing new, nothing had changed; it was the same old story. Nothing changes when a leaf falls from the tree in the autumn. It falls without causing a haemorrhage, without pain, without regret. The leaf fell five years ago. There was nothing new from my husband's side. What was new was new for me: I was the agent this time, not him. Now I was able to say: 'No – enough', and not to hide the 'no' or the 'enough' like the living dead. I am able to act, to struggle out of the wrong orbit until I no longer feel the need to say 'no', to pronounce the 'enough', sterile, incapable of taking action, bitter as the sloe that I chew over in silence, in weakness and in self-loathing. Now I am able to try to reconcile my thoughts and feelings, my dreams and my reality, what I want and what I do. The rift that separated what I want and what I do closed. I thrashed myself to make it close, and the marks of the whip are still on my back.

How could I come to explain to people that my husband, given what was new and what was not new, what he did and did not do, was no longer – and had not been for a long time – involved in the battle. How did I explain that the battle was, above all, my battle to be restored to life after a long barren spell, so that I could exist again, act, take the bull by the horns, be involved in life as I used to be, that the battle was to get out of the orbit I was in and which I knew in my bones was wrong, to put an end to the rift between what I say and what I do, between what I believe in and the reality I live?

I did not explain, I did not reply, but I did not back down from fixing a date to finalize the divorce in my presence and that of my husband in the office of his brother, who was a lawyer. I was determined to go with my elder brother, Abdel Fattah, so that he could pull out the thorns, stroke away the pain and dress the wounds. We arrived at the appointment we had made to the minute and my husband did not come. I waited, as I was used to doing, but this time waiting was not a torture, it was just tedious. Abdel Fattah said: 'It's hard for him and, of course, he's just putting off what he can't face up to.'

(My brother was as gentle as the breeze. He passed away in May 1973, aged fifty-four, eight years after my divorce, in June 1965.)

I waited. He turned up, looking smart and elegant as he usually did, and he asked to be alone with me, to dissuade me from asking for a divorce.

As I followed my husband into an empty room along the hallway, I ran into a lawyer who had been a colleague of mine in the Students' Movement in the forties. I had met him in the office a few times and given him the polite smile which had become mine, spoken to him in the schooled tone which had become mine, looked at

48

him with that look which goes straight through people without seeing them which had become mine. But this time I felt a camaraderie towards my former colleague that I had not felt before. Our eyes met as they had never met before and blazed with the flame of recognition. As I dragged my footsteps behind my husband, I wondered: where did my outspoken ways go, my warmth and enthusiasm when I met my colleagues?

I sat politely on the edge of a chair with two cushions, my legs together and my hands folded in my lap. He sat on a swivel office chair, near me so our eyes would not meet while we talked. We were being, as we had been for thirteen years, extremely polite, extremely civilised, as we were under all circumstances, even when one of us was seething with jealousy, hatred or rejection of the essence of the other. Once, I shouted at him: 'I hate you,' and I slammed the door in his face as I left the room. But that was in the beginning, the very beginning, before I lost myself in him, before my existence hung upon a word from him, upon a look from his eyes. Like the tip of the sword my words were; they could not yet cope with exploring cowardly paths and they were not yet weighed down with fear of getting involved with others and with life, or refined by my sense of guilt and sin. That was in the very beginning, before I masked myself and adorned myself and pretended to be civilized, that was before I was drawn into the frame of the picture in which he imprisoned me.

'It isn't you who's doing this, you're above these trivialities.'

I announced, calmly and firmly, as I sat politely on the edge of the chair with the two cushions, that I was determined to finalize the divorce. He refused to believe that I was serious about going through with it right to the bitter end. Everyone refused to believe it. I was breaking the pattern that I had set for thirteen years with which, it had seemed to everyone, I was happy. More important than that, I was breaking the pattern that prevails in many marriages. My sister said to me: 'All men are like that.'

A friend and colleague called up and read out a statistical survey by the American researcher Kinsey which finds marital infidelity in 99 per cent of marriages in the United States. A brilliant journalist and novelist commented on my divorce in *Akhbar Al-Yawm* newspaper, without mentioning names of course. He said that some women who have a Ph.D. fail the elementary certificate when it comes to being a wife, and it was me whom that great Don Juan was talking about. I resolved to remain silent in any case, as the matter was deeper and more complicated than could easily be explained. Infidelity was not what concerned me. Perhaps it was for a while, but it no longer is. My existence was what was in the balance. I stood at a fresh starting point, where all the close ties there were between me and my marriage, all of them, were severed. Nothing remained when he said: 'I made you.'

He said it to try to win me over, hoping that I would back down at the last moment and not finalize the divorce, but this was not to be. He accepted that things were over when I said, assuming an air of great self-control so that I would not fail to do what I set out to do: 'Even if you did in fact make me, as you say, this does not give you the right to kill me.'

After the divorce, a professor asked me: 'Why did you marry him in the first place?' and I replied: 'He was the first man to awaken the woman in me.'

My whole life began to be evaluated by others. My marriage had perhaps provoked more uproar than my divorce, for my husband and I stood in two opposing camps, even if I was not aware of the fact at the time. Perhaps I was aware of it and ignored it, as I ignored many things. Perhaps I was not aware of it at all and the current just swept me along, swept me away, while I was unaware of anything beyond my quest for the happiness for which I longed. But I was aware that opinion was divided over my divorce. Opinion was divided between those who held existing social patterns sacred even if they were corrupt and those who dared to destroy corrupt patterns, whatever they were, between those who shared my husband's political ideas and those who were against them. (Our political orientations count for a greater part of our temperaments and opinions than we imagine.)

In the fray of the divorce, I refrained from discussing the reasons for my divorce. Every time the subject was raised, I cut short the conversation before it began with the hackneyed phrase: he's the best of people and so am I, but we don't get on. On purpose, I refrained from taking part in the campaigns of abuse that were launched against him in the wake of the divorce. My silence made some of those who were close to me angry. I was determined to remain silent, however, perhaps because in denying my former husband I was denying years of my life, denying myself. Perhaps also, I came to realize, it was because I discovered as I broke the last of the threads that tied me to him that hatred was the other face of love. I took care not to hate him, to destroy all the bonds that remained by escaping from the snares of hatred.

As we waited for the camera to be prepared for recording in a studio at the television centre a long while after my divorce, a Nasserite broadcaster said: 'People understand why you divorced him, but why did you marry him in the first place?'

Her question caught me unawares and the reply I gave without a moment's thought surprised me even more: 'Sex brought the Roman Empire down.'

We laughed together at the ironic detachment of this

remark, or, to be more exact, at the sense of abstraction that my direct reply to her question contained. My reply, true in part, was not the whole truth. But what people thought of my marriage and my divorce was not what made me nervous the moment the camera was turned on me. Deep in my mind, the nagging question remained: have I really been able to get him right out from under my skin?

I went to great lengths consciously to pluck out the remnants of my husband from my being, assessing the experience of my marriage objectively, making the connection between the general and the particular. I split the woman I am into two parts, one that is dying and one that flees in distress, as in 1966, the year after my divorce, I wrote a play entitled *Buying and Selling* that was never published.

Suddenly, my husband fell from my emotions as if he had never existed and, with him, the play I wrote that had seemed to me, in the shadow of the way events developed, pure heresy as the 1967 defeat knocked me down and marked the dividing point between two phases, two lives. Words became emptied of their meanings, all words, and wrapped in the cloak of history and economics I seek in facts shelter from words, all words, head bowed and eyes cast down for fear of meeting other people's eyes. I am the soldier, martyred, not knowing from where the betrayal came; I am the soldier coming back naked in the fevered heat of the sun across the Sinai desert; I am the one who arouses sorrow; I am the object of ridicule and every joke that people tell hurts like an arrow in my heart. O my God, how many arrows you have showered upon me as I dragged on in my failure, my rancour and my desire for revenge as words lost their meanings, all words. What I have suffered as an individual dwindles away to nothing compared to what people as a whole have suffered. I do not exempt myself from responsibility: how did I not say 'no' more often than I did? How could I have been so ineffectual? A few days after the defeat, the Fiction Committee at the High Council for Culture held its meeting, which was attended, quite unusually, by about fifty eminent writers. I said: 'Every one of us is responsible for this defeat. If we said no to wrong whenever it was done, we would not be faced with defeat now.'

The hall tensed as I spoke, some accepting what I said and some rejecting it. Dr Hussein Fawzi protested that nobody was able to say no, and anyone who did would find themselves in prison. Insisting that we take responsibility for the defeat, I replied: 'If all the intellectuals said no, they wouldn't be able to put us all in prison.'

There was a crucial moment of silence and someone asked: what happens next? Still caught up in their dreams, the leftists – including myself – were expecting another Vietnam. Tawfiq El-Hakim said that Abdel Nasser was not better than the Prophet, prayers and peace be upon him, and suggested that there might be a peace treaty like the one Mohamed made at Hudaybiyya. He told his version of the story, right up to the moment when the treaty was to be signed. Mohamed paused as he went to sign and instead of signing himself Mohamed the Prophet of Allah, as he usually did, he just signed his name: Mohamed ben Abdel Muttaleb. El-Hakim captivated us with his story, telling it as only he can, and I realized that the story was a fake only as I stood in front of the iron gate at the High Council for Culture. The truth slapped me in the face: the most miraculous thing about the Prophet was that he was illiterate. He never signed his name. I felt the weight of the betrayal when the Secretary of the Socialist Union said, in a meeting she held in the University College for Women, that the Israelis had come into Sinai like rats into a trap and were fated to die there. My heart sank. I felt choked and unable to breathe.

My brother Mohamed, who had come back from abroad on 6 June 1967, dragged me out of the ground-floor flat where we were taking shelter and, in the dark, whispered in my ear. I did not know why he was whispering when nobody else could hear, until I realized that what he was saying could be said only in a whisper: 'The Egyptian army has pulled back to the Suez Canal.'

Refusing to believe that everything was over so quickly I said, in a tremulous voice: 'Perhaps it's a plan to draw the enemy in.'

My brother Mohamed shook his head. The pounding of his heart rose to my ears and I could not bear the droning sound of his words. At that point, words lost their meaning. Like a wounded animal in search of shelter I went up the dark stairwell to my room, where I shrouded myself in a blanket on the bed. Like salt the unbroken stream of tears hurt my eyes. Weaving flimsy threads, I pushed the knowledge away from me and hung it from them so it did not touch me, fled from the burden of a truth heavier than I could bear . . . When I heard the voice of El-Quwani asking, in the name of Egypt, his voice choked with tears, for a ceasefire in the United Nations Security Council, I realized there was nowhere left to run to and I burst into tears, wailing hysterically. My brothers, Abdel Fattah and Mohamed, as torn apart as I was, tried to calm me down. My sister's husband, Mohamed El-Khafif, said: 'She's right.'

He would have liked to be able to burst out crying as I did. He wept without tears and I threw the cigarette lighter at the television screen, as Abdel Nasser backed down in his speech to Zakariya Muhieddine. Lowis Awad said to me: 'What legal right does he have to do that?' The legality of Nasser's assigning power to a successor preoccupied him as he strolled around his room at the offices of *Al-Ahram*. It seemed to me that his preoccupation with this legal point, when the boat was sinking, was not relevant in the least and appeared to be a way of skirting the main issue. I did not realize until later on that Lowis Awad had grasped the kernel of the whole problem: by what legal right was all this going on? Mohamed El-Khafif asked what the television set had done wrong when the lighter whistled past it, then he and I set off, without saying a word, and picked our way down to the side street in the dark.

In our quiet side street, we found other people feeling their way like us in the dark, some still in the clothes they wore around the house. When we reached the main street, a bus pulled up next to us. The driver had decided to go to Manshiyyet El-Bakri, where Abdel Nasser lived, so we took the bus to Qasr El-Aini, near the People's Assembly, where thousands of people were gathering.

I found myself in the street again, among people, after having been away from them for a long time. The street was not the street I had known in the days of the revolution, and the people were not the same. This time I found myself in the dark, wounded like the others, weighed down like them by doubt, not knowing where we were going, our future enveloped in a thick, unwelcome darkness.

With the greatest difficulty, we found our way to the People's Assembly by the back door. I found my brother Mohamed Abdel Salam El-Zayyat, who was the General Secretary of the People's Assembly at the time, drafting the resolution that the Assembly had published at dawn that night, entitled 'We Say No to Gamal Abdel Nasser.' Mohamed El-Khafif and I helped El-Zayyat draft the resolution, which took some time. We left, past four in the morning, after he had read it out by candlelight in the main hall and the Assembly had passed it.

No sooner had I thrown myself upon my bed, torn apart, exhausted, than I found myself sitting up suddenly, a question eating at me: was what we did right? I threw myself back on my bed again. What other choice did we have, now that the time of questions without answers had begun?

I did not cry the night Gamal Abdel Nasser died. My mother set a pile of handkerchiefs in front of her as she watched the television and everyone cried, but the defeat of 1967 was with me, and the Black September massacre of the Palestinians. I was gripped by bouts of sharp, conflicting feelings. A mixture of sorrow and anger made the tears freeze in my eyes, and a blend of regret for today and fear for tomorrow kept me until morning, waiting for what I feared, although I did not know precisely what the true nature of this was.

I did not hear about Abdel Nasser's death until the news was broadcast. Abdel Nasser was laid out on his bed, dead, as the eye doctor darkened the room and shone the light in my eyes. O my God, how long has the light been piercing my eyes? The doctor shone the light in my eyes and began to talk about the financial problems he had with his wife to a mutual friend, turning to my eyes from time to time, then plunging in to enumerate all the clothes and pairs of shoes he had bought for his wife as the light shone in my eyes. In a nightmarish trance, I fancied that the world had stopped and that I would die in this chair, with the light shining in my eyes. Abdel Nasser is in his shroud on his bed, dead, and the light is trained on my eyes. What is harsher than light in the eyes? When I came home and my mother told me the news, the pile of white handkerchiefs stacked up in front of her, I did not cry. I cried days later.

I stood on the balcony of our house, looking out at a gathering of wailing women dressed in black, confused men, children howling out the death of Abdel Nasser as they beat their breasts. Tears sprang to my eyes as I said in an audible voice: 'Nobody, whoever they are, has the right to orphan a people.'

1963

Plan for a novel

The story is that of an individual in decline, who flourishes in the beginning and who is imprisoned in a cage at the end. He flourishes in himself, as such, is open-hearted, gifted, sensitive, receptive, full of the joy of life; he enjoys every moment, is generous and understanding, forgiving, untraditional. He has faith, believing in something greater and more important than his individual existence, and enjoys the ability to love and be loved.

The main point again is that we do not attain our true selves unless the self first melts into something outside the limits of this narrow ego. (A hint of the main theme of the novel *The Open Door*, which I published in 1960.)

We lose this true self when we become limited, imprisoned in a cage, hovering over the ego, when we drown in a sea of vanities, caught in an eternal vicious circle which turns into our destiny and our end. At that point we lose our selves, not in a metaphorical sense, but actually. Our personalities suffer alarming changes, to such an extent that we become not ourselves. Hatred, not love, becomes our dominant feeling, and tradition comes to the rescue of the individual who has lost his morality and his free moral rules. The individual becomes small and despicable, envious, condemning of others, morally prim, in the worst sense. This sort of person flourishes when he finds evil in other people, as if its existence gives him self-confidence, or the confidence that he alone is rightly guided and the others are not.

The reason for this change (I write and cross out what I wrote; I am unable to explain the reason for a change like this, so I find myself keeping an eye on the symptoms).

The symptoms of change become apparent in a loss of interest in the outer world and gradual enclosure in the petty needs of the self. (It seems I remember that I am writing a plan for a novel at this point.) We have to find a justification for this change in every individual case, I write.

The fault that leads to the fall of a character such as this is a general tendency to choose the easy way out. The easiest way of all is to do nothing, and not get out. Life scares a person like this and he does not want to get involved with it again, nor is he able to. He imagines every time he makes a concession that he has chosen peace of mind, but it is only a temporary peace of mind and one that, in the end, leads to his being afflicted with paralysis or a total inability to move and act.

1950

From a book entitled *In the Women's Prison*

The book tells of my experience in solitary confinement that lasted for months while I was under investigation in the City Prison in Alexandria, as it also shows the sort of regular women prisoners whom I met in this period. The piece that I have chosen is entitled 'My friends' and is the final chapter of the book.

I finished writing this book in 1950, immediately after I was set free, bound over to cease activities, accused along with others of belonging to a communist organization that was trying to overthrow the system of government.

The book is numbered and classified, ready for publishing. It was not published, at that time or at any other time. I ask myself, why was it not published?

My friends

Can I write of my experience in prison without re-
membering you, my friends, who transformed the
nature of this experience, who touched its grim darkness
with white and changed it to a shade of grey which,
although gloomy, was bearable?

Can I forget you who were my guard, when it was you
who turned my loneliness to companionship, transformed my exile to a home? How can I forget, my friend,
the day they cast me into prison, under the shadow of
terrorism, assigning me an alien, dangerous role, then
whipped up clouds of obscurity and ambiguity around
me, invented stories about me and told you: 'Watch out
for her, this one goes off like dynamite, blazes like
hellfire, slips out of your clutches like water; she's been
trying to escape for days, so don't let her out of your
sight, and don't let her speak to the other prisoners as
she's got a tongue like a spout that pours out dissent and
rebellion wherever it can.'

When they saw you narrow your eyes in disbelief as
you looked at my face, they said: 'Don't let that sweet
smile deceive you, she's a wolf in sheep's clothing, and
the sweeter her smile, the more evil she's plotting.'

You looked at my face after they had left and in the
end you said: 'I don't know who you are, but I know you
only wanted to do what was best.'

You were able, my dear friend, to brush away the

clouds they brought down around me. You were able to get straight to the truth and see that I was a straightforward, ordinary young woman who only wanted to do what was best.

From that time on, you stood by my side. You were a strong friend in times of distress, when things reached crisis point and I was cut off from my friends and loved ones. When I think about what you did for my sake – and what did you not do for my sake, Sitt Aliyya? – I feel your kindness swathed around me and I save it up in my heart, unable to repay it and happy because I cannot. I want your kindness towards me to save me for ever, whenever I am gripped by the bitterness of life, from losing faith in the human soul and all the love, nobility and beauty there is to be found there.

Do you know what this human love can do, my friend? It transformed a loathsome building, full of bitter memories, to a Kaaba of Mecca to which I make a pilgrimage, transformed it to a shrine for which my heart aches. That day I longed for you. Enjoying my freedom, I came from Cairo to Alexandria and went to see you in the City Prison, where you were on guard duty. I went on foot to the solitary wing in which I spent the worst days of my life. As I approached the prison building, I thought I would be swamped by a bitterness that would stir clouds of tears to my eyes. But instead a brilliant love glittered in my soul, scattering all bitterness from it as I, the hateful building and the whole universe around me were swathed in love. Nostalgia urged me to walk on into the prison.

Can I forget you, my other lovely friend, whom I snatched up and held the day they threw you into the inferno, whom I loved like a mother although there was not much difference between us in age. When you first came, you found prison very hard. No sooner had you found your own feet than you came to my help with your

61

tenderness. In prison, we became an indivisible unit shaped by thought, opinion and sentiment, and you became closer to me, more rooted in my heart, in my thinking and being, than anyone had ever been before.

When things reached crisis point for us and the dismal news was coming in thick and fast, making our black shadows still darker, you raised your lovely voice in defiance and sang gently in French: *'Demain le printemps fleurira.'*

Can I forget that you stood by me, my friend, when I left the prison in the dead of night, fearing that my execution order had been signed? The political police opened the prison in the middle of the night and a wave of insane terror swept over the prisoners. The 'lifers' swore that such a thing had never happened before, not even for an execution. As soon as it became clear that it was me they wanted, the whole prison rang to one cry: 'Courage!' It seemed to me that the very walls were encouraging me to get up and I did get up. Above all the voices rose yours, my friend, addressing the woman who was able to sacrifice herself. 'Courage, comrade,' you said, and I grew brave. Your voice stayed with me after I left the prison and as I was getting on to the train to Cairo, when I discovered from some colleagues in Cairo prison that I had been invited to attend the trial of my husband and a colleague of mine who stood accused with him and who had asked me to testify to her innocence. I testified and returned to the City Prison, wounded and bleeding.

You had waited for me while I was away, and although they told you I would not come back, you kept the apple your mother sent you so we could share it when I did. I did come back, having felt fear of the unknown and of the known, after the court sentenced my husband to seven years. In court I sang your song, our song, and in your embrace I wept. In my solitary cell, I wept for a long time, and when my tears had dried I sat down to eat.

Here we are, my friend; wherever you are now, we are out of prison. Spring has not blossomed yet and hope has not left me, nor has the song:

> Some day
> Spring will blossom again,
> In a free, free land,
> Where we can live again,
> Where we can love and be loved again.

1962
From an unfinished novel entitled
The Journey

. . . Hide me, mother, hide me. I am ashes, I am nothing, I am a monster with four eyes. In darkness drape me. With slumber in oblivion shroud me. I have put an end to my quest. It's no use, no use.

In the darkness I will lie down and I will not say no. In blackness I will be swathed, in a whisper I will wrap my voice so nobody hears me; I will never raise my voice, with cork I will line my shoes and pass along the winding corridors of the old house as if I were not really there, the corridors will not echo to my footfall. And I will clean my room and clean it again. I will not be content . . . my room is as clean as if nobody were living there, the mirror does not reflect my breath and there is not a single hair of my head on my pillow . . . I will wash my body as if I were washing an ineradicable sin from me, and I will wash it again. I will not be done . . . my face shines like a mirror and my hands are pale; I no longer sweat. I wrap the rough towel around my body and scrub myself with it. The last tremor that remains in me trembles and I wrap the towel tighter . . . The towel is not rough enough, the towel is no longer rough. On the table I pile my necklaces, my rings, powders and scents, my costly belongings, my fine belongings; with my hand I touch them, over my cheek I run them. I take shelter in my bed and I dream . . . my belongings have doubled in number, they have grown many and indistinct in the drawers in the corners on the cupboard under the bed.

I placed my hand on the bottle top with the pointed teeth and took shelter in my bed. I no longer dream. I dreamt my youth and my middle age and I no longer dream. My head is heavy and my eyes shed tears for no reason. I fastened my hand on the bottle top, no longer feeling anything. In the morning they will find the teeth of the bottle top sunk into my flesh and no trace of blood; the dead do not bleed . . . She died a short, sweet death, the death of the chosen, they will say. They will never know that in the old house died her youth and her middle age . . .

20 October 1973

The realization comes to me late, perhaps the tranquillizers dulled my wits, my senses, perhaps the
transition from pathological depression to revival is one
the dimensions of which cannot be known. Perhaps it is
because a realization such as this comes only at a
moment when one is intensely agitated, when all the
joyous moments and the tortuous, the moments of
triumph and rout, despite all the twists and turns they
take, are gathered, honed, sharpened and intensified in
the rising line of a graph.

Were it not for 6 October 1973 I would not have felt
the desire to write these memoirs, or a desire for
anything. I know that my political background has been
transformed with the passing of time to ways of acting
and feeling; it has saved me from some personal pitfalls
and from all the political defeats which Egypt has
suffered and which I, as a consequence, have suffered.

'Nothing destroys me,' I said after I had shaken off my
second marriage.

'Nothing destroys me,' I said after the defeat of 1967,
although for months I beat my breast, saying: 'This
defeat happened to me on a personal level and it is the
hardest thing that has happened to me.'

Only a minority understood the import of what I was
saying and many dismissed my words as a pose, just a
pose. But I also know that my political upbringing and

my entire inner self was of no avail in what happened to me during the year 1972–3. During that period, in April 1973, I lost my sister's husband, my friend and colleague Mohamed El-Khafif, who died suddenly, and my brother Abdel Fattah, who died in May 1973 after a long illness. I was destined to engage in a losing battle with death, the absolute of absolutes, and to become acquainted with forces other than the social forces with which I did battle and which battled with me, in the shape of death. I tried, I tried very hard to get over the loss. The Students' Movement of 1972–3 encouraged me to try, time and time again, as I clung defeated on the brink of the bitter pit.

One day, a colleague, a sweet, loyal, kind friend said: 'I know how cruel the things that are happening to you are, but I beg of you, do not let these things defeat you.' A tremor of fear crept through my body. I leaned on the desk and said, the feelings suddenly taking shape in my head without any advance preparation: 'I sometimes feel as if death has me surrounded.'

I was not speaking that day about death in the abstract sense and it was not fear of my own death that kept me awake at night. It was fear of losing the ones I loved who were still left.

I realize suddenly that I have passed the crisis now or, to be precise, since 16 October. I remember that date because it was the day of Taha Hussein's funeral and the day Sadat announced that Egypt was prepared to accept a cease-fire. But this was just another of those days which began with 6 October and sent me hurtling among people. I live moment by moment, now tense, now happy, one moment lifting me, light and intoxicated, to heaven and the next bringing me down shattered, with broken wings.

On the evening of 16 October, as I sang with hundreds

of other people for today and tomorrow, war and tilling, earth and the salt of the earth, in a stage production written by Samir Abdel Baqi, set to music and song by Adli Fakhri, the sense of finality and despondency that had been troubling me all day left me.

As I paid my last respects at Taha Hussein's funeral, I felt as if I were paying my last respects not to a man but to an era: the era of the secularists who dared to question everything, the era of the intellectuals who practised what they preached and imposed free will on all kinds of oppression . . . Despondency got the better of me and I was tormented by a sense of finality. The sound of the students' voices singing the national anthem, *'Biladi Biladi'*, rose on the University Bridge as the funeral passed.

Reaching out for a helping hand that I already knew would not be extended, I leaned over and asked one of my colleagues: 'What does Taha Hussein mean to a young man or woman of twenty?' She shrugged her shoulders and said, with regret: 'Nothing . . . nothing at all.' Then she added: 'Perhaps *Al-Ayyam* would mean something to a minority, but only to a minority.'

I was shaken by the grief of finality and the way the song *'Biladi Biladi'* turned on the students' tongues to the chant, *'La ilaha illa allah'*, There is no god but Allah. The bridge, packed with hundreds of people, seemed at noon like an empty desert crying out for rain.

I came back from the theatre that evening delirious, even though I had seen the same show for three nights in a row. I was aware precisely that it was the desire to be among the greatest possible number of people that had brought me back after having been cut off from people for so long, and aware that this desire was an urgent need and was my salvation. But, weighed down with doubts, I did not stop to wonder why I was happy when the struggle, which I wanted to be a total war of liberation, was on the point of coagulating again in the poisoned swamps?

I sit in the waiting room of a hospital in London near Harley Street, where my brother Abdel Fattah is undergoing an operation to get rid of a malignant tumour in the colon to try to stop the disease from developing. I sit there, having gone from hospital to hospital with my brother. The prayers offered at the small feast at the end of Ramadan can be heard in Agouza Hospital. There is no prayer for the great feast in the London hospital. Autumn is over and winter has begun.

I asked a nurse for a tranquillizer. How did I forget my tranquillizers today? I took one and sat down to wait. The operation lasted two hours, during which time I was either in the toilet or reading the daily papers. I was not pretending to read, I forced myself to read and I read. I could not make my body do what I made my mind do and my bladder rebelled, vomiting up urine every five minutes on average. My tears did not flow until the moment I had confirmed that my brother had come out of the operating theatre safe and sound.

The door of the lift giving on to the operating theatre opened. I was not aware of it as it opened. A bed came out from the lift doors with my brother lying on it, and I was not aware of it as it came out. I was reading. A Greek woman waiting for someone of hers to come out of the operating theatre said, in broken English: 'Isn't this one yours?'

I ran off after my brother, shrouded on the stretcher in the purplish-pink operation gown, his pale face paler. The nurse stopped me from going any further. Since the bed was at some distance, I shouted: 'Is he all right?'

The reply came in the affirmative and I sat back on my heels to wait. When I reached the waiting room, I burst into tears as I leaned against the door. I had to stop my tears, so I stopped them . . . this round was not over yet.

A week after the operation, as I was looking forward to returning home, with my brother cured, the surgeon asked me to come and see him.

In a sharply drawn circle of light, the English surgeon – a tall, slender man, handsome and self-confident in a stern way – sat behind his desk. I sat, plunged in darkness, on the other side of the desk on a January evening in 1973.

There was a moment of silence as my eyes hung on his lips, waiting for him to pronounce judgement on my brother's life. His death? I leaned on the edge of the desk in search of some light, a little light. The dazzling light shining on the face of the surgeon made me afraid. He sat comfortably in his chair, his fingers twined together, well established in his room and he said, with finality: 'I give him between three and six months.'

'I give him,' I repeated to myself. This third person, this absent third person, does it refer to my brother? 'I give him.' Is this the way Abdel Fattah, my brother, is rendered absent, made abstract? Is this the way my brother, absent, abstract, is lost? Does this man not know how these words affect me? And who is he to give and take away? He is not a god, I said to myself. One side of me is belying the other; the naked truth takes me unawares and makes my hands shake on top of the desk. Something in my expression, my posture, must have moved the surgeon to compassion from his height and made him lean over the desk towards me and speak.

'We've done all that we can do to help him. The disease is not localized, as we thought before we operated. The tumour has spread from the colon to the kidneys. And the lungs. As was clear on the last X-ray.'

I asked, in a voice which sounded like someone else's, about the possibility of medical treatment and if there was a specialist centre anywhere in the world that had success with such treatment. The surgeon said, without mercy, that he thought the possibility of medical treatment succeeding with my brother quite unlikely.

I heard myself asking: 'Will my brother suffer?' The surgeon said that was not likely, and added: 'He'll fade gradually until he vanishes.'

I felt a little easier and I relaxed in my seat, catching my breath. For months after I marvelled at the creature I was from that moment on and up to the end of the interview with the surgeon, especially since I later broke down in the loneliness of my room. I asked the surgeon to make the necessary arrangements for medical treatment in the measured tone which had come back to me. When he protested that it was no use, I fixed my eyes on his face and said: 'Look at it with me this way. We, his family, do not want to torture ourselves with false hopes, but we also want to feel that we gave my brother all the help we could.'

When we had agreed to begin the medical treatment, the surgeon leaned back in his seat again and said: 'There is something I want to discuss with you. The hospital administration has noticed that you are concealing the nature of the patient's illness from him. As doctors, we believe that the patient has the right to know, first of all, the nature of his disease and, secondly, how long he has to live. We usually leave the final decision up to the patient's family.'

I replied calmly and with an air of finality: 'No. No, I do not want my brother, or anyone but me, to know.'

By this I meant my sister and brother. My sister was still living through the shock of the sudden and early loss of her husband, and my brother Mohamed had just survived a stroke and was still getting over it.

When the doctor stood up to shake my hand goodbye,

71

I found myself saying before I left: 'I hope that your future patients are given the opportunity to live.'

For months I tossed and turned in my bed, muttering: 'The surgeon is not a god.' Something was giving the lie to me. The rheumatic pains I suffered in my joints medical examination proved were not organic at all, but they kept me awake all night, muttering: 'The surgeon is not a god.' None the less, I was still annoyed by the entreaties that rose to the heavens, asking that my brother be cured and that he live long.

A doctor friend drew me gently aside from Abdel Fattah's room in Agouza Hospital to the balcony, over which the burning summer sun of Egypt was spread, and he said: 'Medicine is no use to him any more. He'll go into a last coma soon.' He then added: 'Nothing but the human touch remains.'

The coma had begun when I asked my sister Safiyya and my brother Mohamed to go back to the house. They dragged their heels, protesting that they were waiting for spare oxygen pipes, waiting for the end of the glucose injection that a trainee doctor was giving. Breaking down for the second time that day, I shouted: 'Go back home, both of you.'

My sister, enacting the sudden death of her husband a few months before and her brother's anticipated death in the same scene, gave a running commentary as she followed, step by step, his swift decline. My brother Mohamed stood there, his face flushed, as if all the blood had drained from his body and was trapped in his head.

I took a hold of myself after my brother and sister had left and realized that I had to do as my brother Abdel Fattah wanted without breaking down. I felt embarrassed when the young doctor took away the glucose apparatus and quietly left the room, for she had witnessed the scene unfold to the end with the eye of a stranger . . .

Before he lost consciousness the three of us hovered around the bed, asking my brother Abdel Fattah, who had his eyes closed, if he wanted anything. He opened his eyes and his gaze – pure, tender, reconciled – settled on us, one after the other, as he said: 'Thank you . . . thank you . . . thank you.'

I fell on to the edge of his bed and kissed his hand for a moment as he closed his eyes again. I thanked him for being a brother, a father, a companion, for teaching me, for guiding me, for everything. Keeping his ability to control himself, his calm, his dignity, his dry humour, right to the end, he gave me a reprimanding look and said: 'What's going on, Latifa, are we going to stage a play or what?'

He closed his eyes for the last time as he said, making a gesture that went beyond the room to those outside it. 'Courage.'

When my brother and sister left the house, I busied myself supervising the meter of the oxygen tank, quite unnecessarily, to check that it worked, wiping the beads of sweat from my brother's face, putting the oxygen mask back whenever it slipped, turning guests from the door. I broke down in tears in the arms of the one who was closest to Abdel Fattah. I had heated, whispered conversations with Radwa – Dr Radwa Ashur – who was sitting waiting in the adjoining room. I was certain that she would stay as long as I stayed, and I did not try to get rid of her.

I said: 'I'd like to be able to spare you the experience.'

Radwa protested: 'Why do you suppose that everyone but you is a child who needs you to look after them? Don't you realize that you also need to be looked after?'

I patted Radwa's shoulder gratefully and plunged into

a long, fevered, whispered conversation. I asked Radwa after a few days: 'What was I talking about that day?' I could not remember a word of what I had said.

Radwa sighed and said: 'You were telling me how your father died.'

Swept by a wave of the self-pity which I usually loathe, I said: 'I was destined to lose my father twice over.'

I discovered how false this was later, after I suffered the most intense pangs of longing for Abdel Fattah. During this time I realized that the comparison I had made was unfair, for my father was not a companion on my road, and the unique relationship that grew between my brother and me during his long illness was never there with my father. The barriers between my brother and me fell, the gaps were bridged and, after having been a father to me, he became a son, a friend, someone to talk to, someone whom I could ask for advice, and my spoilt child all at once. I stayed up at night longing for him and I would awake to find his shy, happy smile, awake to find that I had gained a new day, another of these unique days of mine, and that the rare, many-splendoured relationship which enriched me when my brother was there, and still enriches me now he is absent, had grown deeper.

In any case, my brother's will obliged me not to fall apart, even if I did realize more with each passing day how heavy a burden this was. I did whatever work had to be done within the narrowest limits possible with that deceptive, self-controlled appearance, my lips relaxed and imagining that I was smiling; uttering words and imagining that I was getting through, making noises and imagining that I was laughing, moving and imagining that I was making progress, reading and imagining that I was aware of what I read, until the day came when signs lost their sense and meanings lost their names. I began to lose the ability to concentrate, and thus to read; I stammered when I spoke, and meanings and names were wiped from my memory – not as if they were on the point of surfacing but were not quite breaking through, but as if they had never existed.

My friends cried over and over again: 'Shed your mourning, move, go out, see people.' I was not able, psychologically, to shed my mourning clothes. I did not wear mourning out of respect for tradition; it was an expression of an inability to live.

I did not shed my mourning clothes until the third day of the October War, after I heard the tale of how Magdi was martyred, on the tongue of Tawfiq El-Hakim, at a meeting of the Fiction Panel at the High Council for Culture. On the first day of the war I was terrified and switched feverishly from station to station on the radio, as the 1967 defeat was still alive for me. On the second day after the crossing, my delirium was contaminated by apprehension and I did not fully grasp the fact that the crossing had been made until the third day, when I listened to the tale of Magdi. Afterwards, I was seized by the desire to go out to people, to be among the greatest possible number of people, to feel confident, to feel that I belonged, as if it were I who had brought the good tidings to Egypt. After that day I heard dozens of stories of heroism, but the tale of Magdi seemed to be the piercing light that gave depth and anchor to dozens of rays of light. Perhaps this story constituted a starting point for me, which shifted things after it in an imperceptible way and transported me, without my being aware of it, from a pathological state of depression to recovery and then revival.

In any case, despite the serious crisis I went through before and after the death of my brother Abdel Fattah, I did not consciously feel the desire to die which I felt the night he died. That night, I envied my brother his death, his body bowed under the weight of the struggle against his deteriorating condition and his accepting, with dignity, the end of the struggle. That night, death seemed endlessly easy and beautiful to me, as each breath my brother took followed further and further from the one before it, and his face took on that calm, which I had never known before, the calm of one who exists and does not exist at the same time. Lines from a poem by Robert Louis Stevenson, 'Requiem', which I had memorized in my early youth, kept repeating, insistently, in my head:

Home is the sailor, home from the sea,
And the hunter home from the hill.

Magdi was not long at sea and he did not want to come home. He was twenty and, naturally, realized that he would die the moment he decided to nose-dive his plane into the Israeli enemy's main orientation building, but his decision was a positive decision not negative, a step forward not backwards, a move outwards not a return to the womb.

When I had got over a serious illness, my former husband commented on the fact that I had been repeating the phrase 'I don't want to die a negative death' while I was unconscious. He said: 'Don't play with words! How can a man die a positive death?'

I meant that I did not want to die willingly fleeing from problems. I did not attempt to explain that death can be positive. He was never touched by passion, by love in the mystical sense, and it is impossible for those who never have been to understand that death is not in the dictionary of the lover or the mystic, for the tree of love is both the lover and the beloved at once. The tree of love does not die. Death is not part of the struggle of the lover who lives in the skin of people as they live in his skin and who, because he does so, does not vanquish

76

death and is not defeated by it, but dwindles and vanishes into the moment of union with the divine, a moment when a leaf of the tree becomes the tree. Magdi was a lover.

They advanced, wave after wave . . . We opened fire on them and they kept advancing . . . We turned what was around them to hell and they kept advancing . . . The canal was scarlet with their blood and they kept advancing.

General Gonin
The Israeli Commander of the Sinai Front

Part Two

1981

From El-Qanater Prison, 1981

1

I came out of Giza Security Headquarters on my way to El-Qanater Prison in the middle of the night, at about two in the morning, on 8 September 1981. I had been arrested a few hours before in my flat. I found an open truck waiting for me, with ten soldiers from the Central Security Force, armed to the teeth, wearing helmets and body armour. I had to squeeze on to the front seat between two officers, along with the driver. They said it would be like this only for a little while, then after a few minutes we stopped in front of the Dokki police station, opposite the Sheraton in Galaa Square, and one of the officers got out of the truck. I don't remember if the second officer stayed or if another one came to take his place; I don't remember who went into the police station and who stayed, or if the one standing on the pavement, swapping papers with the one sitting next to me and keeping an eye on the truck until it moved, was the one who had been sitting next to me before or another one who was higher in rank. I felt cut off from what was happening the moment I ascertained that I was on the way to El-Qanater Prison and that I was going to be slapped about in police stations, for I have had painful experiences in those places before. The feeling stayed with me until the moment I turned my head and looked straight into the face of one of the soldiers sitting in the rear of the truck. The officer was standing on the pavement, supervising the beginnings of the final stage of the journey. Behind his professional mask, the investigator's mask, he was stifling a mocking laugh at all that had happened and all that was happening, at Anwar Sadat and at me, at the order that Sadat had issued to restrict the rights of 1,500 people opposed to Camp David, at himself, at the ten soldiers armed to the teeth guarding a woman of fifty-eight years old. Before he gave the order for the police car to move on to the Women's Prison at El-Qanater, his contempt for it all looked out, barefaced.

He rapped his knuckles on the helmet of one of the ten soldiers and said: 'Open your eyes, you're on a dangerous mission.' He laughed, and I almost laughed with him but did not. I riveted my eyes on the soldier's face and I did not laugh, I choked down my laughter as my gaze settled on his face; no expression showed on it as the officer's hand came down on his helmet and his words rang in his ears. I expected him to make some reply, even if it was dull, but he did not reply. I expected him to make some physical or mental reaction, swift, medium, slow. He did not react. I expected that he would tremble under the weight of the officer's hand, that he would smile, that he would turn pale. That he would be afraid, that he would be angry. He was not. It was as if the investigating officer were talking to someone else, knocking on someone else's tin head. The soldier's face was the face of a man half asleep and half dead from hardship, hunger, abjection and misery. I felt a physical sense of terror that turned to anger as my eyes moved from face to face, the soldiers' faces with their tin helmets, for they seemed to be turned from some half-world, between the world of the living and the world of the dead. I added another reason to the hundreds I already had for being opposed to the regime.

A shudder ran through my body as the truck moved off

and the officer's laughter came echoing back, as the car crossed Galaa Bridge and went past Kasr El-Nil to the Corniche. My sense of being cut off came back as the car reached the Agricultural Road that leads to El-Qanater Prison. The questions the officer directed at me did not make me feel any less cut off from what was happening, or make me wish to draw out the rope of conversation. I was unaware of the presence of the police officer sitting next to me, not even interested in looking at his face as he asked me about the political activity which had led me to prison. I mentioned my activities in the Committee for the Defence of National Culture, which was formed in 1979 in the wake of the Egyptian–Israeli peace treaty and operates through the National Unionist Rally. I was not even surprised at his lack of political awareness when he asked me if the NUR was Ibrahim Shukri's party or Khalid Muhieddine's.

Now I have separated myself from the framework which has been imposed upon me. I am in a car with no driver, out on my own for a drive by night, relaxed, self-sufficient. The grip of the heat and the grip of the government loosen as the car glides, swift as a miracle, through the still of the night, through the crowded streets of Cairo that are empty now, as every pore of my being opens up to the breeze of an autumn night after a long, tense spell that started on 5 September, when the campaign of arrests began, which included my brother among thousands of others and, eventually, me. The car steals on to the broad expanse of the Agricultural Road and end up on the road to El-Qanater as the ancient trees on either side of the road embrace; splashes of light fall through the branches and dance, rippling, on the road and the air smells of clay, of earth, of jasmine and tamarind and of the familiar dams, the barrages from which El-Qanater takes its name. My childhood is etched on that road and in its gardens and so is my youth, the mischievousness of childhood and dreams of revolution, the beginnings of love stories that never came to anything and revolutionary songs, side by side with the President's holiday home from which the order for my arrest, and thousands of others, came. The ancient trees spread their deep roots out and cling to one side of the road, covering the surface of the earth, splitting it open as the new roots are drawn in after the old, striking, stretching back into the depths of the earth whenever the earth spits them out.

I am complete, in harmony with the whole. The car stops and the police officer, who has lost his way, looks in vain for the road to the prison. He looks for the road and I sit back in my seat, filled with exultation as I realized that I behold my freedom, entire and undiminished, at the end of the road. There it is, after all the beatings I took when I was lost on the path I found as a young woman, all the beatings I took to find the path again, all the beatings I took when I lost myself and after all the beatings I took so that I could find myself again, as I lost and found my voice. On the brink of sixty, here I am, sitting comfortably in the still of the night in the front seat of a police car while the police officer looks for the prison so he can deliver me. Nobody can imprison me any longer. My freedom appears to me at the end of the road, entire and undiminished, waiting for me to put out my hand to take hold of it, and the tears which did not fall before fall now, as my freedom appears to me at the end of the road.

At the door of the Women's Prison at El-Qanater are two ancient trees, one of which is more than 100 years old. In the middle of the prison's inner courtyard is a third tree. If I had not had to wait at the prison door, I would not have noticed the two trees outside, but even if you never came close up to it and despite the iron bars in the way, you could not miss the tree in the middle of our prison. Perhaps being in prison, looking at the tree from a distance, behind iron bars, is what makes you suddenly realize why this tree and none other stuck in the mind of the artist Inji Efflatoun, why she painted sixteen pictures of it during the five years she was detained at El-Qanater, as the distance and the bars settle in and the tree takes root in your consciousness.

Each day, the roots of the tree in our prison stretch out into the depths of the earth, each day they creep over more of the earth and the tree rises up, above all the walls. Today – and I have watched the tree from behind the bars for two months – I know that the roots have reached the place where I stand and where I sleep in what used to be, before the detention order was made, the beggars' wing. The roots of the tree in our prison strike deep, the earth closes around them and spits them out and the roots coil up on the surface where they multiply, renew and coil deliriously; they split open the earth and the new roots are drawn in after the old, striking, stretching back into the depths of the earth whenever the earth spits them out.

One moonlit night, as I watched the tree from behind a door made of close-set iron bars, my ears suddenly pricked up. I could have sworn that I heard the distant sound of sap flowing from the roots to the branches to the red flowers, even if I could not say for sure whether what I heard was sap flowing in the tree or blood flowing in my veins. I felt shaken by the moment, then the pounding of my heart drowned out any other sound.

I used to sit on the other side of the tree, in front of the bolted doors where political prisoners used to be kept before the arrests, when the prison was not so crowded as it is now. The political prisoners who were here before and those who came after us sat there; the years come and the years go and they sit there, they come to know the prison and it comes to know them. From here, I cannot see the prisoners in front of the trees. I wonder, how long they have been living in rooms with narrow iron doors – maybe for months, for years, since the moment the first human beings strove to re-create the world and create themselves.

After the pallor that the sunset leaves behind, after the breeze has refreshed the stifling air, something is there which breaks down all barriers; something stretches out threads to the outside world that join up, that tie up, that wrap up the sorrows of our corridors and prison cells and bring a sense of warmth and belonging in their place, threads that bring moisture to what is parched and join what has been sundered, that break our isolation and cast us, roaring with life, out of our cells. I wonder as I look at the prisoners in the rooms with iron mouths, despite the series of barriers and the locked doors, have I ever been imprisoned in the cell each one of them occupies? Is my pallor mine or theirs? The question seems less important as I hear the blood flowing in my veins, clamouring for the love of life, with the will to create a better life.

It was after 3 o'clock, at dawn on 8 September 1981, that the police car stopped in front of El-Qanater Prison and the officer and the assistant constable rapped on the big prison door. The officer went inside and the assistant constable came back to lean on the door of the car where I sat, waiting. The ten soldiers sat in the rear of the car, with their weapons and helmets and armour, just as dull at the end of the journey as they had been at the beginning. As he leaned on the door of the car, the assistant constable asked me about my work and I replied, briefly: 'I'm a professor in the university.'

He said, aghast: 'Oh, good grief.'

The blood drained from my brother Mohamed's face

when the police car stopped in front of the bare door of Tora Penitentiary, the door between two worlds, and he said: 'Why this prison, exactly?'

I had gone with him in the police car from Ras El-Barr, where he was arrested on the morning of 5 September, so that I would know where to find him and also I could learn from the administration of the prison they were taking him to about getting food and clothes to him and what the visiting times were, and so on.

When the car turned off from the Nile and headed for Tora Penitentiary, I thought we were on our way to the old prison, so decided to wait for the information I required in the café next to the prison, on one side of the little square, instead of by the prison gate. I spotted the old prison, as the car went further and further away from the Nile. I thought the journey was nearly over, but it seems it had just begun, as we left every trace of civilization behind and went deeper and deeper among the graveyards, where a few women, cloaked in black, were scattered, making their way to a stony desert that stretched as far as the eye could see, its expanse cut only by this rough, zigzag road with its high bends and by the gateways of the military police, whose barricades broke every stage of our journey as we wound our way through endless desert labyrinths, broken only by gaping holes filled with rubbish and the wrecks of old aeroplanes. The endlessness seemed to fade away as the road, carved in the rock, rose up.

Trying to keep my voice under control, I asked: 'Where are we going?'

The policeman in charge, who was suffering some of the alarm that we were suffering and who also doubted that these labyrinths would ever lead anywhere, muttered: 'To the new prison, Tora Penitentiary.'

The last barrier was lifted to let us pass through to a gate that led on to a courtyard, where there were some buildings which I thought were the prison blocks. When the car stopped, I had to catch my breath, for I saw the highest wall I had ever seen, made of stone and topped with barbed wire, a wall behind which nothing was visible, as if there were nothing beyond it. A wall that separated the known world from the unknown, or perhaps marked the end of the world, or that is how it seemed to me as my brother asked: 'Why this prison, exactly?'

He took out his comb and combed his hair, wiped the dust of the journey from his face with a perfumed handkerchief and vanished behind the wall.

Three days later, my brother had an attack of angina and stayed on the floor of his solitary cell for days. He got over it because he knew the answer to the question: 'Why this prison, exactly?'

On the way back from Tora Penitentiary, the police car dropped me off in Tahrir Square. The policeman in charge did not know that he was setting free one of the people whose names were on the arrest list and neither did I, at that time. I stood waiting for a taxi to take me home and no sooner had I sat down next to the driver, clutching the case of clothes I had brought from Ras El-Barr and heaving a sigh of relief because I had found a taxi that would take me home than I started to feel dogged by the desire to tell. I wanted to tell someone the story of my journey to hell and how I came back, feeling deprived, for what I hoped with all my being was a short while, of the person dearest to me in the world. I stared at the driver next to me for a long time, thinking over what to tell him. The wrinkles that covered his face made him seem a good, kind man and so did the thick glasses he wore that were slipping down his nose. But something in his look, something strange which I can't quite put my finger on, stopped me from talking to him.

After I had said goodbye to my brother at Tora Penitentiary, the policeman in charge said, 'You won't be able to get in touch with him at all now and there are no visits and no food.'

I looked closely at the taxi driver and forgot all about trying to tell him anything. I will not be able to get in touch with him at all now. He looked out from behind the thick glasses, and from the look in his eyes he seemed terrified, afraid of the inevitable crash, guarding against the inevitable crash. The old taxi driver concentrated his entire being into the look in his eyes, a look that pushed death from him and from others, a death that could befall him at every turn in the road. I know for certain that the place for an old man who can hardly see is sitting at home in bed, not behind the steering wheel, and I wonder what pressing need compelled him to take the risk of driving? I said to myself: 'These are hard times, for an old man to be doing this,' and realized that the same thought had been nagging at me that day on two different counts.

I think about the things around me as I sit in the police truck in front of the gate of El-Qanater Prison. I have lost patience waiting for the prison door to open so I can finally settle somewhere I can be certain that there is warmth, however bad the material conditions. There were friends in the prison before me and there will be friends there after me; there were friends here before the detention order was given who have become, because of their imprisonment, virtual landmarks in the prison.

A sound like the clucking of chickens comes to my ears. It sounds strangely familiar and I ask myself, in astonishment, do they raise chickens in the gateway that separates the women's prison from the men's? I look around me to see where the sound is coming from and I see two ancient trees before me, their huge branches crowned with a thick mass of white flowers, larger than flowers usually are. I soon discover that the sound is coming from the trees and that the flowers are not flowers but piles of snowy egrets that settle in the branches of the two trees at night. A warder wearing the official grey uniform opens the door and I feel like calling out: 'Hello, Sitt Aliyya!'

It was not Sitt Aliyya, I was not the young woman I was in 1949 and the prison was not the City Prison in Alexandria. I went into El-Qanater Prison at the age of fifty-eight, certain that the fragments of my life would finally fall into place like a row of pearls strung together and that this could not have happened had I not resumed my political activity, had I not made the woman – mummified, pressed between the pages of a book for fear of clashing with life by speaking out – speak out.

I was the young woman who went into the City Prison in Alexandria in March 1949 and, at the same time, I was not her. I put her aside for a while when I left the rough apricot tree laden with its fabulously delicate white flowers behind me, and the expanse of earth that is Egypt, the passion of the Sufi who dies and is born again in the whole, a song to inspire the people of the East to cast out the tyrants, I put her aside when I left all this behind me and chose a path that was not the path, a song that was not the song and a passion that was not the passion. O my God, how long has this been going on? How did I put aside the woman from the City Prison, and why?

The apricot flower no longer tells me that spring is here, that contrast between the fine, delicate white flower and the rough, bare brown branches no longer plucks me from the whirlpool of everyday life and casts me to wallow, elated, in a new dream. At the trial, when her husband was sentenced to prison in 1949, she sang, imprisoned but free:

Tomorrow spring will come again.
We will love and be loved again.

She sang of a spring that was not hers alone but a season for all, and the love she sang of was love for all. It was a spring that contains all and blossoms in the whole, a spring in which all humanity can love and be loved.

Spring came again, came again and again, and every spring the apricot blossom burst from the rough, bare branches, but the spring of which she sang did not come. Year after year she sang of it with the beat of her heart, with the tip of her pen, with the scope of her imagination, with the splendour of dreams and deeds. She prayed for it by night, sleepless and trembling as she waited for the break of dawn. She prayed for it by day, full of vitality and vigour, her veins bursting with a life too strong to be contained, concerned with the most minute details, full of cares, and still the branches of the tree do not soften and burst into leaf. The apricot blossom splits open the rough, bare branches so it can appear, a dream brought back to life that no sooner appears than it shrivels and vanishes. How soon the apricot blossom fades!

(I know now that one has to water the tree to make it turn green, without waiting for it to turn green. Despite persecution and oppression, I watered the tree. Despite the secret reports, despite the bugs they plant under my scalp and the secret cameras they slip under my skin, I know that one has to water the tree.

In the last ten years I have not seen the tree turn green. Once, in October 1973, I saw the plant put out jagged, rough branches, and I wept for my whole life when they tore the plant up before it blossomed. I knew then that one has to water the tree even if one never has the chance to see the tree turn green.)

How close the spring of love seemed, in 1949, to the

young woman who went into the City Prison in Alexandria. It was a certainty as she ran in the desert of Sidi Bishr, which is no longer a desert, kicking pebbles up high in the air with the toes of her shoes and singing:

> O people of the East,
> The time has come to cast out the tyrants.

The day they arrested her and her husband was right after the Palestine War, when martial law was imposed, when the Arab people responded and the rallying cry that rang out in the campus of Fouad I University was echoed in other throats, in Tunisia and Jordan and Lebanon, when the waves of rebels rose in human seas, their banners the shirts of martyrs drenched in blood. The waves boil, rise, rage, threatening a storm, threatening to reshape things, threatening to bring the eternal spring in which we love and are loved for ever, and so a venal war ensues, declared by corrupt regimes with ineffectual weapons to maintain the iniquitous situation, not to restore the land of Palestine. The blood of innocents flows and the capital of a greedy king grows vast; his iron grip fastens on the nation and the tide draws back from the streets for a while as she sings in the desert at Sidi Bishr, which is no longer a desert:

> O people of the East,
> The time has come to cast out the tyrants.

I feel alienated. The East is transformed into the Middle East to make way for Israel. The Arab people no longer respond and, in a flash, the defeat of 1967 looks out on us. My sense of alienation increases as, in November 1977, after Sadat's visit to Israel, I stand with Abdel Rahman El-Abnoudi saying to myself: I must be mad. I hold paper and pen, begging pardon of my

92

people, digging tunnels to connect us, rebuilding ruined bridges, joining what has been sundered. I could not stand where my people stand and I could not be far from it; it is I who draws my life from the umbilical cord that ties me to it . . . Time passes and smoothes away false consciousness and alienation. I resume my position and breathe. I breathe long, I breathe deep, for the belly of the earth whispers secrets to anyone who listens carefully with the heart and ears. The tide does not come, but the surface of the calm sea seems to sparkle with life, the blood creeps through my dried and wasted veins again, the rupture is mended and what had been sundered is joined.

The woman of twenty-six sings of revolution, inspired by the vision of eternal spring. She has only to stretch out her hand and catch hold of it, to summon it up with songs of revolution, to sing as people save her from the clutches of the police who arrested her husband. She sings on the run as she slips from one strange house to another, for the police have banned her from returning to her own house and her family house. She dances feverishly as her husband escapes from prison during the investigation and the chase begins, for the two of them, as she sings, nervous, afraid, in disguise, in hiding, as she moves with her husband from a house in Sharabiyya to a house in Zeitoun. The chase goes on and on, and ends the day they arrest the two of them in a wooden house in Sidi Bishr with a walled garden and a pond that on moonlit nights turns to a bar of silver, there, where there is material to be printed and distributed, some of which is buried in the belly of the earth, which guards her secrets, where there is an apricot tree that blossoms in her heart always, despite everything, in the darkness and when the darkness fades. If it did not, the darkness would not fade.

*

93

The apricot tree was the last thing she saw as the police car turned with her and her husband, that March day in 1949, on the way to the city of Alexandria governorate, where she spent her first night alone, after they separated her from her husband. She forgot about the apricot tree on the first night in the governorate and on the second night, in the police station at El-Karakoun, although it sprang up within her on the morning of the following day to remain in bloom for ever.

She lost consciousness that morning the moment the door, locked for twenty-four hours, opened. She came round to find a hand patting her shoulder and the face of a man from the countryside looking into her face. She came to her senses surrounded by human warmth, her nostrils filled with the smell rising from four rounds of falafel squatting on a fresh piece of brown country bread and the sight of drops gathered like dew on a glass of iced water. The rough hand belonged to a simple soldier from the countryside whose humanity was stronger than any orders he had been given, whose kindness had upset the plan to bring her to the investigation exhausted. Tears of gratitude shone in her eyes as she shyly reached out her faltering hand to settle on the rough hand, to join what had been sundered, to dissipate or dispel the fear that she might be tortured in the governorate, the cheap victory won by the man with the cruel features, the wind howling through the bars of the wide, bare cell during the night she spent on the asphalt floor, holding back her bladder and bowels, rapping on the door and getting no response, her loss of consciousness, the pangs of hunger, satisfied now with longing, joy, a sense of being reconciled with people and the world, of victory over the man with the cruel features as she sets her hair straight and wipes a wet handkerchief over her face in preparation for her meeting with the District Attorney.

As soon as she walked into the investigation room in the police station she found the District Attorney sitting at his desk with an officer from the political police on either side of him, one of whom she recognized as the man with the cruel features who had made her feel so deeply lonely at the governorate. He was remarkably tall, well built and dark, with a big nose. The other officer's face seemed more generous. (She was young and still put people into pigeon-holes and passed absolute judgements on them. The man with the cruel features had not yet put on the mask that revealed nothing.)

The investigation started. It did not go on for long because they had already found the entire body of the crime of thinking: papers containing ideas written by her, her husband and two colleagues who were there when they were arrested. There was no need for an interrogation; the idea did not need to be drawn out from the coils of the mind to substantiate the charge of thinking, the thoughts were down for the record, spoken out. There was no need for an interrogation. The investigation began and ended. Throughout the investigation, the man with the cruel features mocked her and her husband. Throughout, the man with the liberal features protested against the mockery, attempting to make the burden less and make her more comfortable, telling her that he knew her relatives in Alexandria and would deliver any messages to her family, and bring her food and clothes from them. The District Attorney seemed to be a good man. He ordered her a cup of coffee, which she needed most desperately, and when she raised the cup to drink, the aroma pierced her nostrils like nothing before. After the end of the investigation, he asked if he might ask her a personal question, nothing to do with the investigation, so she gave her permission. He asked: 'Why are you concerned with politics when you're pretty?'

She did not realize that she was pretty, she did not realize it until she met her second husband, so she accepted the compliment with a smile, ignored the fact that it was a stupid question and classified him as a good man, as she did with the man with the generous face who had stood up more than once to save her from the coarse treatment of the man with the cruel features. (He had not yet put on the mask which hides coarseness.)

She was young and did not yet know the rules of the investigation game. She did not know what purpose they served either, or how far promises went, although she knew how far threats did, as she listened to the moans of torture in the governorate in Alexandria. She did not yet realize that kindness and cruelty are an inseparable part of a battle fought to destroy a person's ability to think and that these, in context, can be almost impersonal, if that is the right way to put it. She was young and she did not yet realize that the good man in this context was not necessarily good or that the man with the cruel features was not necessarily cruel.

I knew this man with the cruel features later, in 1971, as the Prime Minister of Egypt under Sadat, when he and I had both changed. When the face is covered by a mask of wrinkles everyone looks like everyone else, they look like one another, so it is easy to change places, even if this resemblance never really did convince me and our positions were never really changed.

After she had spent more than ten hours alone in the interrogation room in the Alexandria governorate, well on the way to morning, he came rushing in looking elated and triumphant. At that time she did not understand why he wanted so much to say what he had to say, or why he could not wait until the morning to say it, but now she does. It seemed to her then that what he said was totally unconnected to what was happening. Nothing appeared to link this man's wild joy with the tortured cries that began to reach her, indistinctly, at the same moment. She did not understand why he was a thousand times more elated by his triumph over culture and intellectuals, 'university graduates', than by being promoted immediately after they had been arrested. He repeated what he had said, indicating her, her husband and their two colleagues. He repeated what he had said and the reference was to all intellectuals. Wild with joy, like bullets he fired his words which destroyed thought, the ability to think, destroyed culture and intellectuals. She waited, impatiently, for the man to move away from her so she could think, so she could think through the terrible battle that might be waiting for her and, finally, he moved away. Her battle made her forget this man with the cruel features completely until she saw him again in the investigation room.

After he left she had to prepare a nervous piece of machinery, highly sensitive to physical pain, for the possibility of torture. The cries of pain began to reach her, connecting up in one big jolt that whipped her body and awakened her mind. The light of her mind lulled her body, purified it, tempered it to steel, prepared it for the bout of torture that she now awaited, prepared, certain of her ability to rise above it and certain that nobody would rob her of the ability to think, to know right from wrong.

The woman of twenty-six imagined, as she entered the City Prison in Alexandria, that she was prepared. Now I know, as I enter El-Qanater Prison, that nobody is ever ready, that one has to prepare oneself over and over again, every moment of one's life. Like breathing, we do not stop preparing and the only tool we have with which to prepare ourselves is the ability to think and to tell right from wrong. I know that people's ability to think was always the target and that imprisonment, exile, threats, pursuit and torture are only ways of robbing people of their humanity or their ability to think and criticize. I know that one is not defeated as long as one preserves one's humanity. I know, as I enter El-Qanater Prison aged fifty-eight, that the investigation is not set for a particular hour or day or year; the investigation begins and does not end.

The eye of the man with the cruel features tries to rob you of the ability to think, but cannot. Now it has become an electronic eye that tries to rob you of your thoughts with sound and image, but cannot. The investigation begins and does not end. The eye of the investigator, like the eye of God, reaches you wherever you are, observes your every move, sitting comfortably in your chair absorbed in a book, bowing your head in concern while you listen to a friend tell you something, stirring your cup of tea with a little spoon in the morning, nodding or shaking your head, stretching out in your bed, tossing and turning anxiously as you throw the covers from you, muttering in your dreams, plunged in sleep, screaming yourself awake from a long nightmare that begins and does not end, soothing away your fears after you have woken up screaming, assuring yourself and the investigator's eye that nobody, no matter how artful and creative they are in devising methods of torture, can rob a person of the ability to think.

2

The woman at the beginning of her second marriage was a different woman from the one she was at the end of it, and during both these phases, she was different from the woman who entered the City Prison in 1949 and from the shy young woman who began at Fouad I University in October 1942. No doubt some line draws together the many faces of the one woman who is me, a line that joins these scattered points to the moment I entered El-Qanater Prison in 1981 at the age of fifty-eight. As I entered El-Qanater Prison it seemed that it was important for me to find this unifying line, of which I had been dimly aware, as if the political activity which had led me to prison was the real and healthy sum of my life in the face of an oppressive, hostile reality, which one must strive to change.

The woman from the City Prison came up to me one morning after four years of my second marriage and she came to stay as, with the aggression of 1956, I gained back my interest in things outside my second marriage. I began to write my novel *The Open Door* in 1957 and I published it in 1960. In an interview about the novel, which had been a great success, a BBC reporter asked me: 'Why this novel, precisely, at this time?' She was alluding to the hostile tendency in the novel towards the British Occupation but the allusion escaped me.

I said: 'I wanted to capture my vision of reality when I was young, because if I didn't it would have escaped me in the end.'

At that time I did not grasp the essence of what I was saying, or realize its importance, but I do now. During my marriage, my vision of reality went through changes that almost wiped out the girl and the woman that I was before I got married. As I wrote *The Open Door* I was – without realizing that I had killed her – breathing life into the girl so deeply involved in student political activities against the British, breathing life into the woman so deeply involved in the clandestine activities, after she graduated in 1946, which took her and her first husband to prison. I was making a public statement, although I was not completely aware of it, that I preferred the path she had trodden to the path I had chosen the day I accepted my second marriage in 1952. Man in this novel does not really find himself, does not become whole, unless he first loses himself in a whole, a totality greater than his narrow, individual self. The open door to true peace with the self is the door that opens on to belonging to the sum, the whole, in thought and word and deed.

The resurrection of the woman from the City Prison in my emotions was not a resurrection in reality and I did not imagine that it would be so easy, after the pro- tagonist had suffered the changes she did; it was the fulfilment of a wish for resurrection on the pages of a book. I thought that if I could complete the book, I would be able to end my second marriage, that I would exist again. That is what urged me on to finish the novel. There were moments, especially towards the end, when I despaired of finishing it; then I did finish it, but without restoring the power to act upon what I had decided.

After the novel came out, a left-wing friend said:

'Everyone who read *The Open Door* was astonished because you have not changed.'

I was dumbstruck. It had not occurred to me that I had changed, or that I had stopped believing in what I had believed in all my life, or that I had changed my allegiances. I knew that the man I loved and had married was different from me and that, over the years with him, I had weakened and given in on many counts, even if I never gave in with my mind and never surrendered the hard kernel, the core of my being, to which I unconsciously held fast. But now I know that, all along, I deceived myself so that the marriage would last. It is true that I did not surrender the hard kernel, where the possibility of salvation lay. But it also true that in the last years of my marriage, a chasm opened up between my dreams and my reality, between my wish to act and my ability to act, between my intellectual convictions and the life I was living, and this chasm left me paralysed, with a sharp and increasing sense that I was somehow in the wrong orbit and that there was nowhere else for me.

After *The Open Door*, I began to write a novel in 1962 which started out with the title of *The Apricot Tree*. I intended to take the police chase after me and my former husband as a framework for this novel, in which the will of the fragile person wins out over every shade of social oppression. I planned to use irony as a structural element, so the chase ends in prison – with failure on a material level. However, this failure is really a moral victory since it is under the harshest of conditions, or despite them, that a person blossoms and that the soft, delicate apricot blossom bursts out from the rough, bare branches.

My choice of this framework for the novel was guided at that time by my growing sense that the most cruel prison is the one in which the individual imprisons himself, and that the most cruel form of oppression is that which is self-imposed.

As I wrote, the title *The Apricot Tree* fell away until it completely vanished from my mind and the novel found itself a new name, *The Journey*, an allusion to the entire human journey from birth to death. Far from the ironical framework I had intended as a structure for the novel, the reality that I was living at that time went straight on to the page. I found myself groping, in the dark, after two frameworks that did not work together: a social framework with characters, individual and formal at once, with an era of history and a geographical setting, and then a metaphysical framework, beyond time and space, which refers to the human journey in its entirety. I went back to this novel time and time again, and time after time I failed to complete it to my satisfaction. It remained a problem for me, since what I had written was the end of a novel, not the beginning. It was only some time after my divorce, when I had restored my view of social and historical reality, that I discovered the root problem of this novel.

The vision of reality in *The Journey* is a painful one – it was mine at one point in my marriage – but strange, given the general direction of my life's development as a whole. In this novel, man is individual, not social, and his freedom is a burden which he alone has to bear. He is an ahistorical individual who finds himself thrown into an absolute, ahistorical situation, and his ahistoricality is brought out more strongly by his endless isolation and loneliness. The other, in relation to this individual, is hell. The individual acts, but his acts emanate from him without enriching him; they lack justification and they transform neither reality nor the self. The act in this novel is born of the moment and gathers no weight; it does not spring from a coherent character with a history, or build a coherent character whose actions extend from past to present and flow on into the future.

Now I know that the price I paid during this stage of my second marriage was high. It shows in the cruel, tortured view of existence which resulted from the sense that I stood alone, in front of a blocked wall, and from my being influenced by existentialist philosophies.

It is fair to say that before and throughout her second marriage, as a girl and a woman, she satisfied one half of her human characteristics at the expense of the other half. This was one of the reasons why the course of her life was distorted.

The girl at puberty felt the kindling of sexuality and, because of her upbringing, because she was serious, she stifled it. Feeling acute guilt, she buried the woman so deep that she was no longer aware of her, or hardly, so deep that nothing of her showed except her shyness about this full, curvaceous body of hers. As the girl weaved her way with difficulty across the reference room in the library of Fouad I University, from the reading area to the bookshelves and back again, with some reference book or other, it seemed to her that everyone in the room had fixed their eyes on her. When she realized she had not found what she was looking for, which meant she had to make the same journey again under those predatory eyes, she felt like fleeing the room.

It is difficult to believe the way this girl developed, two years after she started university, when the National Movement, a revolutionary tide, rose there. She stood up to deliver speeches, her voice ringing out on the steps of the university's administrative building, on the doorstep of the Faculty of Law, in the corridor of the Great Hall, by the statue of the martyr Abdel Hakim El-Garahi, calling meetings and leading demonstrations, confronting the opposition put up by the students from the Muslim Brotherhood. She no longer felt confused by her body, she no longer felt that she had a body. As people literally transformed her, furnished her with a strength that she had never had before, as the people raised her up on their shoulders like a banner, with complete faith in her, appointing her as a thinker and a leader and turning her into a legend, she forgot that she was a woman at all.

When she first started university she felt inadequate, like any girl does, and she became determined to challenge this and prove the equality of women with men. She would get angry whenever one of her colleagues offered to carry her books or stood up to give her his seat in the tram, and she firmly rejected it, because it made her feel inferior to the opposite sex and because she felt bound to prove something.

She no longer needed to prove anything as she sat on the steps of the library, caught up in an intellectual discussion with a group of colleagues, while a colleague from the Wafdist vanguard, who was a member of the National Council for Students and Workers, physically dragged one student after the other to her, asking her to talk to them and convince them to join the ranks of the National Movement. She no longer felt inferior as students put her forward for round after round of free elections until she and two colleagues were appointed as representatives of the General Secretariat of the National Committee of Students and Workers.

From the cloak of contact with the masses I was born and from their warmth and stability I was transformed, from the girl who bore her womanly body as if it were a sin into that tough, liberated young woman, so full of vigorous protest, who knew how to win over the masses, how to resist when they refused and smooth them down again. From the cloak of contact with the masses was born the young woman able to reach out with her hands

104

and quite delirious from doing so, able to face up to things and to sway the masses and bring them round . . . 'My isolation will soon be broken,' she says, and her isolation is broken. The ability to convince others comes to her as easily as breathing; she copes with the rejection of her ideas when they refuse and turns around their refusal, breaks through it, nominates herself and they grant her a name and an identity; she nominates herself, their names come to her and she is wrapped in warmth and strength again.

The young woman acted as a person, not as a woman, in the public sphere and this is healthy. She acted in the same way in her private life, since the demands of political work and the image that people had of her, which she adopted, made this necessary. (When she thinks about it now, it seems to her that people turned her from a person to a picture into whose frame she was careful to fit, a legend that she tried to live. The legend had to be destroyed for her to be able to live, after having become the total opposite of the human being and the woman she was. I hope that this is not a new self-justification and self-deception.)

Lowis Awad said that the Egyptian communists, like the Puritans, live a committed life and it is a harsh one. This was true of the young woman who, among others, headed the National Committee for Students and Workers. It was true of the married woman who went to the City Prison. Until that time, she had been a political person, general sentiment and concerns dominating over particular sentiment and concerns. She chose to marry a colleague when she began university and not the man she loved, because to have done so would have taken her from the political work she believed was necessary.

The image that other people drew of her – and perhaps this was the way she liked to see herself – was that of a serious woman, with a strong sense of ethics, who was committed to the struggle. It was no effort for her to be like that: it was the way she was. Words of private, heartfelt admiration and intimate declarations of love fell without clinging to her, like water off a duck's back. She came out of the City Prison after six whole months of solitary confinement with half of her human faculties engaged and the other half latent, almost dead. She had to move from one extreme to the other, as the woman in her sought revenge for having been denied for so long and fought for the opposites to be reconciled, for the complete being to emerge, an extremely individual person as much as an intensely committed social one. (I hope that I am not justifying and deceiving myself again. All I can say for certain is that this split, along with other shortcomings, was one of the reasons why I achieved so little for a relatively long period of my life.)

The woman at the beginning of her second marriage was the female, called forth like a genie from the void, wiping over what had passed before as if it had never happened, embracing the present and flourishing. Her husband used to ask her all the time: 'Why do I love you so much?'

He used not to like it when she said: 'Because I'm so good.'

She was not provoking her husband, or joking, or being humble; she was very self-reliant, she knew her strong points and listed them all in the column of 'good', which she considered until then the source of all her strengths. Until then, she liked to think of herself as a good girl, serious, intelligent and quick, both sweet and stern, able to win people's love and respect. As the marriage developed, she discovered another way of seeing herself that sometimes contradicted the familiar image. She discovered the image of the woman who is loved and desired, seen from the viewpoint of a lover who wants to express his feelings, desiring to master the art, to excel in expressing his fervour. Her husband had a lot to say and he said it well. Breathless, she listened to him telling her about the curve of her cheek, the tone of her voice, the cadence of her voice, the look in her eye . . . It was as if she had discovered a treasure in herself that she had known and not known was there, and she stepped back in astonishment, timid and confident, embracing her discovery. In the beginning, she dismissed this new image as worthless, laughing at it, disbelieving, but as it imprisoned her, she soon came to worship it.

Now she is concerned with her clothes and grooming, with her jewellery and powders, with quiet pastel colours to match the simple lines of simple, elegant clothes, the only things which suggest the past of a woman who used to think concern with appearances trivial, a ridiculous, bourgeois indulgence, a stupid attempt to conform with corrupt institutions and a corrupt society.

The woman at the beginning of her second marriage was treading a very different path from the one which the woman from the City Prison had trodden. She was striving for a salvation that was not hers, singing the praises of a love that was not hers. She left behind, in her house with her first husband in Sidi Bishr, the shy dance around the fishpond which on moonlit nights turned to a bar of silver, she left behind her sense of camaraderie, of belonging and companionship, of pure, uncomplicated love, the feeling that she was dying of fear and then being resurrected beyond fear, the thrill of danger, of challenge, of soaring above all obstacles. She left behind the martyr's howl of joy, the serenity of the prophets, the expanse of earth that is Eygpt, the passion of the Sufi who dies and is born again in the whole, the song to inspire the people of the East to cast out the tyrants, and she chose to go back to the fold. (I have never thought of describing my second marriage as a return to the fold. I had put it down as having to do with passion, not fear. Did it have to do with both of these at once?) The apricot tree that used to give to everyone no longer gave to anyone but her, and the song of love that used to belong to everyone became her song alone. She became the roots and the tree, the clay, the white apricot blossom and the rugged branches, the singer and the song, the poet and the ode, the earth and everything on it. She was plunged deep into the fantasy of unity with the other. She was young and did not know that this is how one becomes trapped in a bottomless pit, and had the woman she was not come to her rescue, even at the last minute, she would have stayed, trapped, flailing around in the depths of that bottomless pit when she had given up everything, everything but that hard kernel that lay at the core of both women. Perhaps she lost sight of the umbilical cord that tied her to the land and the people to whom she belonged, but it was always there, a line of continuity in her life.

Now I know that the woman from the City Prison was still there in one form or another throughout her second marriage.

Now I know that true love was not the only motive for my second marriage. True love justified everything, it masked the desire to conform, to go back to the old house, to the embrace of my father out of fear and terror, to renounce what had been, to erase it from other people's memories.

Now I stand, fighting for breath, as I realize that it has taken me a lifetime to acknowledge this truth, a lifetime in which I hid from it on purpose, terrified, full of guilt and a sense of sin without knowing what crime I was supposed to have committed. I realize that hiding from this truth for so long was what made me fragile as porcelain, wounded by the breeze, forever afraid of being wounded, forever in the wrong, no matter what the circumstances, and always ready to apologize for being in the wrong when I had done no wrong. Hiding from it made me feel defeated all the time, that I could not do anything, that if I started something it would come to nothing. It paralysed me and, as I became free of paralysis, I was afraid of being paralysed again. Now I know.

Now I know that this acknowledgement must lead me to another, more painful, acknowledgement which will blow away my talisman, my amulet and my charm, the parable in which I sought divine guidance, the one I twisted my head to see in the dark, to be lit up by it in the depths of darkness. Now I know that this acknowledgement must lead me to another, one that destroys my legend, the last of my legends, or I hope it is the last: the legend of the woman who entered the City Prison at twenty-six. I do not mind, I no longer mind. Something in my present is crystallizing that rids me of the need to have a legend, to twist my neck to look back. Something is making me stay happy with myself, able to do without legends, happy and reconciled with myself. I no longer mind as my legend is destroyed, the last of my legends, or I hope it is the last.

Now I know why I insist on seeing her as the woman who went into the City Prison, why I do not see her coming out of this prison. I know the emotional state that made the prison gate signify the gate of the second marriage. I did not feel before that this woman in the prime of her life had been defeated in prison. Perhaps before being sent to prison, when the police arrested her husband in 1948 and she just escaped being caught, when she was barred from her house and her family's house as she fled from the police, spending each night under a new roof, one strange roof after another, as she waited anxiously for the end of the night so she could seek refuge somewhere else. One day during the investigation, her husband escaped from prison and she followed him from house to house and they did not settle in any one place long enough for the house to become a home. They worked night and day, non-stop, as their connections were severed and the decay grew worse, even in the ranks of those who had stayed on the path and had not given up. Her ideals were destroyed and her close ties severed; she kept her ear to the door, waiting for the knock, as the circle narrowed, inexorably, day after day, until the knock came, as she sang:

> O people of the East,
> The time has come to cast out the tyrants.

I never wondered before, was the woman defeated in prison, or even before. I never found the answer to this question. All the signs suggested that she was able to rise above the tribulations of prison, and perhaps they still do: she had a polished image, and still does. The morning they arrested her she tried to escape from the clutches of the police, to melt back into the crowd. One does not escape if one is tired, if one despairs or has had enough and can no longer fight. When they caught her in the middle of the road, she stopped and did not apologize. She was not yet burdened by a sense of guilt, and she had not yet reached the sphere of errors where she must forever apologize, as if for her very existence.

The political police were astonished at how calm and alert she was when she was leaving the house to go to the governorate. She packed a case of clothes for her husband and reminded him to take a toothbrush and toothpaste, which prompted the policeman in charge to say: 'Do you think you're going on holiday or what?'

In the investigation she did not shrink, did not weaken. She had that image of herself and the love in the hearts of her generation that does not permit one to shrink or to weaken.

After prison she wrote down her experience and, it is true, she did not stop crying as she did so. Were they tears to lament the creature that she had been and feared she would not be able to remain? She cried a great deal as she wrote down her experience, although she stopped crying as she divided it up, set it in order, rewrote it, dotted the i's and crossed the t's so that it could be published. In everything she did, this young woman was purposeful and complete, even under the most extreme conditions, for the word is always an act. She had not yet experienced introspective reflections, writings that were not meant for publication, plunging into the depths, trying to understand, to get somewhere just to come up with a handful of air and that destructive feeling standing on the brink of certainty that nothing she does will ever be complete.

She dotted the i's and crossed the t's of her experience in prison so that it could be published. Was that before she met her second husband or after? At the beginning of her second marriage she was still busy with her first book, still in manuscript form, with her second husband's comment written on it: 'sentimental, too sentimental'. Was she preparing the manuscript for publication or was she deluding herself that she was doing so? It is difficult for me to say for sure. At that time she was at the beginning of her marriage, and there was still that distance between them, that way of coexisting independently which allows such a distance. She had that peculiar psychological and intellectual ability to refuse to surrender any of the things she held dear, that ability to refuse, to articulate what it was she was refusing, to be certain that her refusal was logical and had an acceptable justification, that the other was the one who was wrong and that she was right. She was able to stand up and defend what she believed to be right. Was the trance brought on after that as a result of love? Sex? Am I still afraid to call things by their names?

I will never know if she did prepare the manuscript for publication or if she was deluding herself, but she certainly did not publish it. Of course, publishing was not easy and the censor's reservations about printed materials may have made publishing this book impossible. But the fact remains that she did not try.

For years I believed that the book was not published because my present style had left behind what he called its 'sentimental' style which made it no good for publication. I became so convinced of this that I did not go back to the manuscript until years after my divorce. (Perhaps there was some truth in this conviction. I felt the need to find another form to express the experience of the City Prison when I finally went back to it.)

But what concerns me now is, why did I not try to publish this manuscript at that time? Did I neglect to do so because I was afraid, having been bound over to cease all activities, or was it because of my desire to draw a curtain over the past, to complete the act of conforming and return to the fold? Or was it for both these reasons? I think it was for both these reasons, and I realize, after all these amendments, that my acknowledging that the gate of the City Prison led on to the gate of the second marriage means that the young woman was defeated at one point in her development.

I must re-read what I wrote about my experience of the City Prison. As far as I recall, writing down the experience is not a sign of defeat in itself. Perhaps my defeat is hidden between the lines; my writing this experience down on paper must contain the beginning of the defeat. Otherwise, I would not have severed ties where I should not and would not have connected where I should not, where connection is impossible. In order for the connection to endure, we have to be doing what we consider to be right, not what we consider to be wrong.

El-Qanater Prison,
13 November 1981
The Search

I need to think about the experience I went through
yesterday during the ward search and understand it.
Yesterday I laughed at my behaviour, which seemed
strange and made the other women on the corridor
laugh last night, but I am not laughing at it today.

Yesterday's search was not unusual. It was not even
particularly severe, considering the stories they tell in
the prison about the previous campaigns of harassment
on the political prisoners' corridors, of blindfolds and
whips and so on. It was my behaviour during the search
that seemed strange.

It would be easy to avoid thinking about it by saying
that everyone was hysterical and I was no exception. But
it is difficult to reconcile yesterday's hysteria with the
sense of fulfilment that I feel today. It would be easy for
me to say that everyone has their own, distinct sort of
hysteria, but the hysteria that came from me was not of a
single width, did not flow in a steady, unbroken stream.
It was of varying widths and full of contradictions; it
came from worlds that until then had seemed separate
from one another, like forgotten islands.

It had never happened before that the dividing line
between reality and imagination, life and art, had
slipped from my consciousness, or that the terrified
child and the bold girl who found salvation in

belonging to the whole, and the young woman debilitated by the inability to act, and the woman in the middle of her life pressed between the covers of a book to avoid a clash, all burst into life from nothing, at the same conscious moment.

Yesterday, we anticipated the familiar search: the commissioner standing with officers and warders in the courtyard outside our corridor waiting, giving the Islamists the chance to put on their veils. The woman officer opens the bags, puts her hand inside among the clothes in the same polite way that customs officers do, making a search that usually comes to nothing. During the course of two and a half months, we grasped the dialectic of the struggle between warder and prisoner, so we enjoyed our ability to predict the search before it happened and hide everything that had to be hidden.

Although we were mistaken yesterday in our understanding of the way the struggle between warder and prisoner would develop, we brought the clash up to twice its pitch. Although this was unusual, we were expecting the usual reaction.

We had to do something to prevent Amina (Dr Amina Rashid) from undergoing disciplinary steps when she came back in the afternoon from the prosecutor's investigation.

The news leaked to us through one of our sources of information in prison. News was not supposed to leak, so the news, any news, information, any information, whether it was personal or not, or read or heard or seen, from inside the prison or outside it, was kept from prisoners. After Amina left the corridor in the morning she was searched at the gate. They found two letters, one to her husband and the other to her son. They were taken as evidence and sent right away to the general administration of the political police. The prison administration issued a report in preparation for the disciplinary steps that the prison would impose upon Amina after she came back from the investigation.

When we knew what was happening, we were supposed to arm ourselves with the knowledge and pretend, as we did each time, that we did not know, so that the officer designated to our sources by the political police would not be taken away – which would have compelled us to go back to zero and start looking for fresh sources, for prisoners need to know what is going on as much as they need to breathe. But this time we had to do something to prevent Amina being locked up in the disciplinary ward when she returned. If we had not done something, we would have died of anger.

We went with the group from our corridor into the adjoining courtyard, which was also fenced in with iron. Our strike petition declared that the situation would remain as it was until the demands mentioned in the petition were met. The petition bore the signature of two groups of prisoners, which the authorities had presumed would be fighting one another because of their political and cultural tendencies, their way of life and their age. There was one group of people known as Islamists, a group of five girls, and one group to which Amina, Awatef (Dr Awatef Abdel Rahman), Nawal (Dr Nawal El-Saadawi) and I belonged.

The moment the iron door of the courtyard revealed the Commissioner, I realized that he had come intending to undermine the Islamists in order to break the strike. The Commissioner gazed past the outburst that I made with Awatef and Nawal, and hung on the entrance to the corridor, waiting for the women to come out wearing their veils. As I followed his gaze it seemed to me that the entrance to the corridor, when there were no longer any

116

beds there, was like the mouth of some fabulous animal with its fangs removed.

When the five girls came out, dressed in black and completely veiled, the corridor bared its fangs and a look of fear trembled in the eye of the Commissioner as the girls stood side by side in line, a forbidding wall made up of Sabah, who had not been the spoilt child of our corridor but became so after we consciously rose above the possibility of conflict between the two groups, Amal our housekeeper, Nadia our Minister of Supply, Hoda, and Sayyida Zarqa El-Yamama, who predicted danger before it happened.

I sighed with relief when the Commissioner moved on from promises to threats. We waved aside his threats, which lacked credibility, and asked for the letters to be returned. Amina's personal letters assumed a huge importance, the way the Commissioner told it, a way that oppressed me, and everyone in this world and the next. I found myself finishing the discussion by saying to the Commissioner: 'Stuff the letters.'

For the thousandth time, I am astonished as I use phrases which before prison I considered to be sordid street talk, and go beyond it, longing for confrontation for the thousandth time, the woman in the middle of her life fleeing life between the covers of a book.

(Prison turns smooth, white silk gloves to boxing gloves that hit straight at the target; prison reduces one to the basic elements, elements pregnant with all possibilities, so that one could be a stony ground, a green ground, ripe with greenery, fire and water, clay trodden by feet or a piece of porcelain that tells of man's ability to create beauty and to re-create himself. In prison, you became ferocious and beautiful.)

As soon as the Commissioner had left the place, routed, the corridor made ready for the search and did not make ready. Some hid what had to be hidden and some counted on the extra time which was usually given to the women who wore the veil to finish veiling.

I gathered Amina's diaries and my own and I rolled them up and stuffed them, with the pens, in a cardboard box. I left out a copy book with Amina's name on and one with my name as camouflage. I set straight the nylon cover on the radio we all shared. Sayyida stood watch at the outer gate and Sabah covered me with her cloak until I had finished hiding away the things we were not supposed to have.

It occurred to me, as I filled a bucket with water, that my papers were all jumbled up in their secret hiding place and that although I always tried to keep them in order, they were not. I poured the water from the bucket on to yesterday's newspapers, which had been burned in an empty toilet bowl. Sabah thrust a letter from her father into her bosom and announced that she and the letter would part company only at the very end, when they had to. In a festive mood, we spread out in the corridor courtyard, this time sitting on the edge of the beds rather than lying on the floor. We sat, chatting and sunning ourselves, and the dark cloth of the Islamists' veils revealed long robes that screamed out with hot pink flowers.

The emptiness of the corridor alarmed me after I had left everyone stretched out in the sun behind me. I missed the feeling of life aflame with prayers and supplications, arguments, laughter and tears, running races and the girls' youthful games. I looked to my left, where the girls' beds took up three walls on the corridor, and I found only one broken, black bunk bed with the girls' belongings on it. I noticed on the top bed my only dress, a blue winter dress that I had set aside for going to the investigation, that had never been used. I swerved to the right on my way to the lavatory. In the two corners which were taken up by our four beds there was still a cardboard box overturned, which I used as a little table. Under it, I had hidden books and notebooks with some observations which I intended them to find during the search, to draw them away from the written papers which I had hidden close up to the wall to the right of another old bed. On the top bunk of this bed were our suitcases, Amina, Awatef, Nawal and I, and on the bottom bunk were four cardboard boxes, one each, containing small things like a toothbrush, toothpaste, a comb, soap, laundry soap, a plate, spoon, cup . . . and so on. Right next to the bed were wooden shelves made out of an old bed leaning on empty panels on top of which we had piled food – lentils and rice – and cooking pots. In front of the shelves was a gas ring and a stone for whoever was cooking food to sit on.

It occurred to me, as I strolled into the lavatory at the end of the long corridor, how protracted our battles with the prison administration have been and how protracted they still are, so that we can win, time after time, each one of these clauses, so we can attain the lowest human standard of living now that the prison administration has cut off the link between us and the outside world.

In a lavatory without a door, I passed by the long basin with the three taps where we wash, by the wall opposite with the nails fixed in it which we use as hooks for clothes, and the washing line where we hang the underclothes that we cannot bear to be seen by those who enter. I went past the first lavatory, the only one with a door, to the third, unused lavatory and again poured a bucket of water into it so as to leave no trace of the ashes of the previous day's newspapers.

The search began as I sat on a seat with a hole in it, busy in a lavatory without a door. I heard the usual screams that the girls made when a man caught them by surprise, unveiled, and the sound of running footsteps, dozens of them. Strange sounds were mingled with the familiar sounds of prisoners and warders. I listened carefully to make out what was going on in the corridor but I couldn't tell anything. Suddenly, I heard Sabah screaming in the lavatory next to mine. I heard pounding on the door and curses and I found, as I leapt up to help Sabah, that I was in no state to leave the lavatory. To aggravate the warder who was pursuing Sabah, I shouted: 'I'm here! Come on, search me.'

Trying to draw off the pursuit from Sabah, so that she could throw her father's letter that was stuffed down her front into the lavatory and pull the chain, I said it again and there was no reply. A struggle was going on by the only toilet door in the lavatories and there was a final scream from Sabah, then the sound of feet running after other feet. And a silence more frightening than the scream, and a voice other than that which whipped Sabah reaches me, dull and languid, in reply to my phrase with the word 'no'.

When I came out I found the bare backside of a warder leaning with her grey dress over the lavatory, her right arm plunged into the bowl. Handprints painted in excrement colour the wall of the toilet, like handprints of blood to celebrate the sacrifice of a sheep. There is no trace of Sabah.

I pass the bare backside and the handprints of blood, and a plywood door that the butcher's knife tore apart. Terrified, I stand in front of a woman with maimed eyes, with a flat chest and flat buttocks, blocking the way from the toilet into the corridor, and the shriek of the victim is lost in the drumbeat of the exorcism, the ritual of sacrifice, *zar*, and nobody hears, and Rayya and Sakina take me by surprise in the dark of the night in my bed, the child in the thirties, Rayya and Sakina, the most savage killers in Egypt.

I run to my mother's bed, panting, terrified, before Rayya and Sakina strip me, before I scream and the drumbeat of the *zar* and the ringing voices drown my screams, before the butcher's knife flays me and cuts me into a thousand and one pieces and I am roasted by the fires of hell in the great furnace, before I turn into a handful of ash with water poured over it in the lavatory bowl. The police station is in front of Rayya and Sakina's house and there is nobody to help the victim; the police station is at the end of the knife, in the blaze of the fire, in the ringing voices, in the drumbeat of the *zar* and there is nobody to help the victim.

Because I am no longer the child who finds refuge in her mother's embrace from the evils of the world, I wonder as I look at the warder with the maimed eyes, with her flat chest: is this like Rayya in Salah Abu Seif's film, or like Sakina? I move the warder out of my way to the corridor.

I imagine that the shadow of Rayya and Sakina has fallen from me, and it has not.

For a while yesterday, as I stood on the brink between nightmare and reality, I found myself dealing with a savage show of power, as if I were facing a gang of thieves and their leader. The dividing line in my mind between oppression inflicted by those in authority and oppression inflicted by a gang of killers and thieves disappeared. It was making this link, between these two levels of oppression, that I describe as strange behaviour, and it was that which made me and the others laugh yesterday, at the mix-up. And there is no mix-up.

(There is no mix-up. Now I know that I have known this fact since I was a young woman. I hid it away in the furthest reaches of oblivion and now I bring it back.

121

There is no mix-up. The oppression inflicted by those in authority is the same as the oppression inflicted by killers and thieves. I know now that yesterday I was the young woman settling an old account with the killers and the thieves, an account she did not settle herself the day the police bullets felled fourteen people, dead, right in front of her eyes and she did nothing, was not able to do anything.)

The massacre in the middle of the thirties that the young woman saw from the balcony of the house on Sharia El-Abbasi in Mansoura was not a nightmare, it was real. The link that took root in the young woman's mind and joined Rayya and Sakina to the killer policemen was no theoretical or fanciful link: it was the fruit of her own experience.

I know now, as the young woman and the woman at the end of her fifties, that what I imagined yesterday to be some ridiculous nightmare is the heart of reality.

I grasped what was going on as soon as I had moved the warder out of my way. The corridor with the iron door in the middle was divided in two by a row of warders, so that the search could be carried out in two phases without missing anything. The search was now under way in the part which the girls use. Nadia stands there, alone, without a veil and without her black robes. She is surrounded by a group of warders. Women's clothing flies thick and fast and tumbles to the ground. In our part of the ward, next to the lavatory, my colleagues and the rest of the girls struggle with the warders, dressed in grey, preventing them from making any advance on the lavatory or getting anywhere near their belongings. The door of the corridor is ajar and there is no official, man or woman, to supervise the search. I make out the warder, who has her hand thrust into the girls' belongings; it is the canteen official who we deal with daily. I quietly resolve to reach an understanding with her; let us wait until there is an official present at the search.

I break through to where the search is taking place (at that moment, the stories which the prison tells about the moment of madness of the woman who takes off her clothes and stands naked as the day she was born in any battle or scrap slip my mind). I put my hand gently over her hand, thrust into a bag, I open my mouth to speak and nothing comes out. Everything is upset, the search is planned in two phases, the blockade in the ward divided in two and so is my sense of reality.

The warder holds me tightly. Her skinny body, convulsed with madness, turns to acute angles of nerves tense as iron. Everyone is gathering around me now, the warders and the prisoners. I am pushed this way and that by hands that deliver me from the grip of the woman of iron, cast me into her grip; screams of protest and curses fly through my head and, for no reason, the madwoman lets out a long scream, as if it were her last breath. The group scatters from me as it gathered and I hear footsteps running after mad footsteps and I do not know why, or where they are going.

I rise to the sound of short cries of terror coming from the lavatory. The sound of a brawl, a scruffle. I rise to find the Commissioner, planted in the ward since I don't know when, his head thrust into Amina's bag. Their hands plunge now into all the bags; they drop like hawks upon our underwear, our papers, our implements; they seize their quarry and let it fall, violated, on the floor.

My sense of reality is upset as the screams from the lavatory join and gather in a single scream that envelops me and the whole ward. I scream at my nakedness for I have discovered that the only dress I own to leave this hole in has disappeared from where it was on the edge of the bunk bed.

123

'Where is my dress?'

Nobody hears me cry out as the battle carries on in the lavatory and the cry of terror now turns to desperate cries of resistance. More warders have disappeared into the lavatory now and I hear the sound of bodies thumping to the ground, being dragged along the ground, as I cry out again: 'Where is my dress?'

Now I stand face to face with the Commissioner and I feel that my existence depends upon getting back what has been stolen from me. Was it my dress? My humanity? What has been stolen from me? From us? Was it just at that moment, or in every decade past? Now I shake the Commissioner's arm, asking him to give back what has been stolen. I am not put off by the look of surprise in his eyes or by the alarm in the eyes of the warders as I shake his arm in a frenzy.

My sense of reality comes back as a grey wall of warders forces the girls back along the ward like captives, in the presence of the Commissioner, stripped of their cloaks.

Now I know that I was the girl who, in the middle of the thirties, went down from the balcony to Sharia El-Abbasi in Mansoura and scuffled among the yellow buttons and the dull-black rifles. I know that I was the young woman who, in the middle of the forties, sat on the edge of Abbas Bridge, her salt tears turning to stone as she waited for her companions, drowned one after the other, waited for the corpse of one companion after another, covered with the green flag, the victims of the Abbas Bridge massacre.

I began to pick up the girls' cloaks from the pile, their gloves, veils and scarves, while the battle raged. The girls kept seeking refuge in the lavatory, time after time, to veil themselves, and I kept going back and forth across the ward, coming and going to the lavatory. To each I gave something of her own – a cloak, a headscarf, a veil, gloves – and went back to carry on looking through a huge pile of clothes, medicine, towels and broken kitchen utensils. On my third trip, carrying two cloaks, I noticed that my things were being inspected and my most private possessions were flying through the air. I felt a wave of anger as I carried on with my task. On the fourth trip, as the parts of their outfit came together bit by bit and the girls covered themselves up again, as things reached completion, I felt that the search no longer concerned me at all and that nobody has the power to strip me or get under my skin.

My eyes weep as I finish what I am doing. I drape the last cloak over Sabah and hold her to my breast, the salt tears in my eyes that turned to stone are spent, the tears in the eyes of a young woman who sat on the bank of the Nile in 1946, watching one person after the other drown.

I headed for the door that led from the lavatory on to the corridor. It seemed like a narrow passage, rough and dark. I went past the heaps of things that littered the passage, the devastation and the darkness, then I opened the door as wide as it would go and slipped out into the courtyard and the sunlight.

It crossed my mind, as I settled comfortably on the end of the bed, that I could now put my papers, that were all mixed up where they lay in their secret hiding place, in order.